ELDORADO

The City Of Gold

L. Norman Shurtliff

authorHOUSE®

AuthorHouse™
1663 Liberty Drive, Suite 200
Bloomington, IN 47403
www.authorhouse.com
Phone: 1-800-839-8640

© 2007 L. Norman Shurtliff. All rights reserved.

No part of this book may be reproduced, stored in a retrieval system, or transmitted by any means without the written permission of the author.

First published by AuthorHouse 11/26/2007

ISBN: 978-1-4343-2426-9 (e)
ISBN: 978-1-4343-2425-2 (sc)

Printed in the United States of America
Bloomington, Indiana
Library of Congress Control Number: 2007906772
This book is printed on acid-free paper.

Contents

Chapter 1
       Lima – Modern Day   1

Chapter 2
       Present Day – Lima, Peru   11

Chapter 3
       SPAIN – 1528   17

Chapter 4
       Atlantic Ocean 1530 - Off the coast of Panama   23

Chapter 5
       Panama City -- 1525   29

Chapter 6
       Present Day Lima, Peru   39

Chapter 7
       Tumbes 1531   43

Chapter 8
       Cajamarca 1532   51

Chapter 9
       Spanish Controlled Cajamarca - 1532   59

Chapter 10
       Lima, Peru – Modern Day   69

Chapter 11
       Pisaq, Peru….Present Day   81

Chapter 12
       Cuzco—Present Day   93

Chapter 13
       Cusco, Peru - Modern Day   103

Chapter 14
       Inca House Restaurant – Present Day   113

Chapter 15
       Cusco – Present Day   127

Chapter 16
    Cusco Restaurant – Present Day   139

Chapter 17
    Upstairs in Monica's home – Modern Day   149

Chapter 18
    Cusco Restaurant – Modern Day   161

Chapter 19
    Martin Hacienda, California – Modern Day   165

Chapter 20
    San Francisco Airport – One Week Later   173

Chapter 21
    University of California, Berkley – Later that night   179

Chapter 22
    Martin Ranch – Present Day   193

Chapter 23
    Berkley, California – Present Day   205

Chapter 24
    Lima International Airport – Present Day   215

Chapter 25
    Lima, Peru – Modern Day   231

Chapter 26
    Lima, Peru – July 26, 1541   243

Chapter 27
    University of California – Present Day   251

ACKNOWLEDGEMENTS

First of all, this book is my own doing and responsibility. If there are any errors, they are my fault. I don't pretend to be perfect or even an expert on the subject of Colonial History or even the life of Francisco Pizarro. I am, however, an avid reader and lifetime lover of the history of South America. My sole interest in writing this book is to promote the fabulous history of this wonderful people.

I would also like to take this opportunity to sincerely thank all those individuals who have believed and helped on this project. Thanks I give to my wife, Christal, for her love and support through the years. I have truly been blessed beyond measure. There have been many who have read and lent suggestions to the manuscript. I thank these people for their friendship and valuable contributions to the finished product. And last of all, a big thanks goes out to the publishers and marketers who wanted to publish a book written by a poor country farm boy. Thank you…….L. Norman Shurtliff

DEDICATION

This book is dedicated to my wife, Christal. She is the love of my life and mother of my children. She is a romantic at heart and we have traveled the lands of the Americas together. I dedicate this work to her because some of the adventures contained within these pages we have actually survived together. I love her forever, and this work is dedicated to her.

PREFACE

What prompts a poor country farm boy from Southern Nevada, transplanted to Canada, to write a book, any book? It isn't money or fame writing to a limited audience. It is really simply a love of the land of South America and a people. Their history needs to be told in more abundance and celebrated. This book is a poor and humble attempt to bring their heritage to life, and I hope the reader will come to love this people, their land, and their history as I do.

Modern city of Lima today as it sprawls along the coast of the
Pacific Ocean

Chapter 1

Lima – Modern Day

The School year just ended for the University of San Marcos, the largest public university in Lima, Peru. Monica had gone through graduation ceremonies the month before, but had to stay in Lima for the last few weeks to finish exams and to pack up and clean up her apartment. Monica was looking forward to returning home to Cusco. Her uncle, Carlos had offered her a fantastic job as his Deputy Director of Tourism. The job didn't pay as well as she would have liked, however, but she had to start somewhere, and this was still the best job that anyone in her class would receive upon graduation. The government jobs in Peru were notorious for being very low paying, and most government employees usually had to look for second and third jobs on the side just to make ends meet and to pay all the bills. So, in fact, Monica was very fortunate to receive such a good job right out of school, but it was really because of her uncle and his connections. And Monica was very grateful for his assistance and the opportunity he was giving her. She had promised herself that she would do the best of her ability to really live up to the trust that had been placed in her. Monica was also looking forward to seeing her mother and to finally be home once again. It had been five long years, except for the occasional visit during holidays and school breaks, since she had been able to return to her beloved Cusco. Monica had spent the last few days packing and saying goodbye to all of her friends in Lima. She sat on the edge of her bed looking into her bedroom mirror. Where had all the years gone? Monica was now twenty-three and she was still the same girl that had left her home at age eighteen. She had grown up a lot and she wondered how much things had changed back home. As she gazed into the mirror she realized that her dark black hair was now a little bit longer. She styled it differently to give her a more mature business woman look. Her eyelashes were longer and she had learned to use less makeup, but accentuate her good features better than when she was younger. Monica just stared at the young woman looking back at her, and smiled. She liked what she saw. "I wonder if even my own mother will recognize me."

Monica had boarded her express bus early in the morning. This six o'clock bus was an express that would go directly to Cusco, making the trip in only 18 hours. The express only stopped for the occasional coffee breaks and meal time stops. This luxury bus had a hostess, a bathroom, and two drivers for the long trip. It was the nicest and newest bus that Monica had ever been on. Even the large fabric seats, which reclined to allow the travelers to sleep comfortably, smelled like they were brand new. Monica had phoned her mother and let her know that the time of arrival of the bus into Cusco was estimated to be around midnight. Her mother had promised to meet her at the terminal. The next day would be Saturday and her mother had alerted all of their relatives and friends of her arrival. A large feast had been planned along with the largest party ever seen in downtown Cusco. At least, it would be the greatest fiesta amongst the proud traditions of the Rodriguez family in the last few centuries, anyway. They were all proud of Monica and her accomplishments. She was the first woman in her Peruvian family history to ever finish university.

Yesterday, she had shipped by truck all of her earthly belongings back to Cusco. It gave her a bit of a melancholy feeling to be leaving Lima. She had come to love the sun and the beaches. She would not miss the eight million people, the smog, and the huge dirty city that sprawled forever. Monica had made many friends, dated a couple of guys seriously, and had made memories that would never be forgotten. This was what really would haunt her and made the University experience here in Lima so poignant. She had grown up here. She had grown from a young teenager into a self assured and confident woman. Monica knew that she could tackle the world and win the battle of life. Lima had taught her that. She had refused to get discouraged when her money had run out; and she had been forced to work part time, as a waitress at a very upscale restaurant in San Isidro, a suburb of Lima, while going to school. Monica just used the setback as a motivating factor to drive her forward in her chosen field of tourism. She treated every customer as a potential tourist or client that she could serve and impress. Monica's smile and demeanor were legendary at the restaurant. Her boss had been forced to increase her hours and pay consistently because of the comments of the restaurant's patrons. So, after three years of loyalty to her job, her boss had staged a surprise going away party two days ago for her. It was the first time that she had ever seen the crusty old grouch ever cry as he hugged her goodbye.

It took an hour and a half to actually leave Lima and its traffic congestion even at six A.M. The bus took the express way route out of the city to the north along the coast toward Nazca. The Pan American Highway passed through barren desert with sand dunes and with very little vegetation. This bus trip from Lima to Cusco would be an exhausting and grueling twenty-two hour experience. What started out to be a large modern toll freeway soon became only a narrow two lane paved highway. The express was making very good time, and the passengers that hadn't gone back to sleep this early in the morning were excited to be started on their journey. The bleak dry landscape was a stark contrast to the jubilant and talkative conversation that was prevalent onboard the bus. Every few minutes an oasis patch or line of green vegetation and palm trees was evidence of a stream or river that was winding its way down from the Andean foothills to the Pacific.

Monica had dosed off. She had stayed up late doing some last minute packing and cleaning. In reality she couldn't sleep because of the adrenaline rush involved in finally going home. So even when Monica had forced herself to go to bed, she had slept poorly anticipating getting up early to make it to the bus depot on time. Monica was now sleeping so soundly that she didn't even notice that the bus had turned east and inland. The course through the foothills made the elevation increase rapidly. Several times the turns in the road were so sharp, that the shoulder and head of the small elderly lady sitting next to her, fell on to her shoulder. The older woman was obviously more tired than she was, but this little annoyance didn't even bother Monica at all as she slept. By the ten o'clock rest stop the coastal desert had already given way to the lush verdant green hillsides and valleys that were part of the famous Andean countryside. Monica awoke with a start as the bus came to an abrupt stop….it was the ten o'clock rest stop. As Monica got off the express bus, she could feel the change in climate already. The oppressive sultry heat of Lima was now replaced by the cool breezes of the hill country. Monica lifted her face skyward as she descended from the last step to the graveled parking area. The cool temperature and the fresh air smells brought back memories of Cusco and home and she was at once homesick all over again.

The bus driver hurried everyone back on to the bus.....it had only been twenty minutes, but Monica was anxious to get going again, too. In an hour the bus began to make some very steep grades up into the mountains. The highway became narrower and employed switchback engineering to help make the mountain climb possible. The sharp turns on the switchback curves made it impossible to go back to sleep and Monica felt nauseas anyway. It didn't really help to look out the window because of the sheer cliffs on her side of the bus frightened her immensely. Monica was suddenly glad that she had paid the extra money to go on the luxury express bus with air conditioning as opposed to the smaller slow, and older buses.

"Bam.....Bam" there was a deafening loud noise, and a noticeable jerk and quick compensation by the driver to get a handle on the bus's sudden erratic behavior. The driver was swearing rapidly and passengers were yelling and screaming, and many were standing and trying to look out the windows. They had been hit and sideswiped as the bus had come around the last of a series of switchback curves. In the back window an old blue station wagon car of a late 70's vintage could be seen. It was speeding away down the mountain road. Now, the attention of all the occupants was fixed on watching the commotion between the driver and his partner. Frantic swearing and curses filled the front of the bus. A wide bend with a turn off appeared and the bus came to an abrupt stop. After a couple of jack knife turns forward and then backward, the driver had managed to turn the big express around and point it back down the hill. Now, the rage on the driver's face could be seen by everyone on the bus in his visor mirror. Fear and terror was Monica's first emotion that was quickly replaced by disgust.

The bus was picking up speed and it seemed that little care was being taken for the welfare and safety of the passengers. The bus was careening down the mountain out of control and the driver's only concern and fixation was the old blue car far ahead of them. Monica found herself screaming and shouting at the drivers to stop the bus immediately and let everyone out. No heed was taken. The driver was fixated with his passion…hatred and rage had completely overcome him. Monica closed her eyes and just slumped in her seat fuming….she wasn't frightened anymore just plain mad at the driver. She had seen this macho behavior before. It was freely exhibited by her last two boyfriends and a good reason why she was still single. Monica couldn't stand this male chauvinistic attitude that seemed to dominate the behavior of the Peruvian male species. Time after time the bus nearly either collided with the mountain side or went over the edge of the cliff. It was nothing but a small miracle that they had been chasing down the mountain for thirty minutes and were still alive. By now, the old blue wreck was aware of the big express bearing down on it and the station wagon had picked up the pace as well. Even though the car was old, it was much smaller and could maneuver the turns better and at a higher speed. Twice the express almost hit oncoming buses in its panic to catch up. It was lucky that it was close to lunchtime, and the traffic was more sparse than usual. Now, other passengers were also yelling to the drivers to slow down. Women and children were crying and frightened, and the bus had its own mutiny brewing amongst the upset passengers. Nevertheless, the bus continued downward, hell-bent to catch the offending car. A slow moving produce truck caused the car to slow and within minutes the traffic had backed up enough that the bus had finally caught up.

The rabid driver first tried ramming the car in front of him. When the station wagon would not pull over, then the driver tried another tactic. The bus driver swerved around the car, but crammed the steering wheel quickly back the other way and narrowly missed an oncoming car. Again he tried to get around the station wagon, but had to quickly get back into his own lane for another truck. A third time the driver swerved into the other lane. This time he was too late because the blue station wagon had already accelerated and was passing the old fruit truck. The express bus was quick to follow suit, and the high speed chase was on again. The whole bus load was once again yelling and screaming in fear for their lives.

The express bus driver narrowly made the next curve and the bus's occupants were now cowering down in their seats with their heads down and clutching to the arms of their seats and holding tightly to stay in their places. Finally, on a straight stretch the momentum of the huge bus going downhill sling-shotted the bus past the station wagon and then immediately slowed down. With the oncoming traffic the car was forced to slow down, too, and finally stop. The bus driver quickly opened the door and bolted out into the road. He fairly ripped the car door open and had a hold on a small young man who was attached to a frantic young woman. The crying girl had hold of his arm which was ripped free by the bus driver. After a few quick punches, the bus driver was laid out on the ground. The companion driver witnessing his buddy in trouble was out the bus door and to his aid in an instant. The battle commenced and the first driver was back into the fray. It appeared that the bus would end up without any drivers for awhile because the young car driver was obviously up for the challenge.

Monica didn't even remember getting out of the bus. But, there she was actually standing between the two parties of combatants…Monica was so disgusted with the barbarianism displayed by her opposite sex that it had compelled her into action. She stood there for the next ten minutes defiantly lecturing the two parties about proper behavior on the highways of Peru. "You are disgusting….aren't you ashamed of yourselves?" The three men with hands and faces bloodied, stood in a circle with her with their heads down, embarrassed, and eyes riveted on their shoes. "What if a tourist from some other country had witnessed such a scene? We are trying to increase awareness of our beautiful country and encourage people to have a good opinion of us and a great experience here in Peru. Aren't you ashamed of yourselves?"

She boarded the bus a final time after they decided to return the scratched bus back to the terminal in Lima, which was now only two hours away.

It was late evening, and Monica was back in her girlfriend's apartment in Lima. Monica had made arrangements to get to the airport in the morning and had bought a one-way ticket for the one hour flight from Lima to Cusco. Monica was so terribly distressed about the events of the day, that she had decided that she didn't want to repeat the same bus trip again tomorrow. Besides her mother had the big party planned for tomorrow night anyway. The only consolation, she mused, was the cheering crowd and the standing ovation that Monica had received from an appreciative bus crowd audience. The bus occupants had actually cheered for Monica after she had reprimanded the drivers and taken control of the situation.

Monica truly believed that Cusco was the most beautiful city in the world. Nestled in a high green valley of the Andean Mountains at 11,000 feet above sea level, Cusco appeared in her airplane window. The capital city of the Incas had 400,000 inhabitants, and was a sea of red tile Spanish Colonial roofs. Cusco was a stark contrast to Lima and its ugly tin roofed adobe houses. Twenty-eight Cathedrals and Churches that are more than five hundred years old punctuated the small cobblestone streets and public squares from her aerial view. The long narrow valley was surrounded by mountains on three sides. Monica was amazed at how the city had grown in the five short years that she had been gone. Oh, how she loved the view in her window....Oh, how glad she was to be finally home again.

Monica collected her two suitcases from the baggage carousal, and headed to the exit. Her eyes searched all the waiting hoards of people. Some of the people were guides who held up signs. Others were taxi cab drivers who bullied in to whisk off confused tourists. Monica just stood her ground and surveyed the rows of people. At last she saw her mother frantically waving her arms and motioning to Monica. Incredibly, a shock wave of feeling came over her; it was like a glimpse of eternity..... deja vu. They ran to meet each other, her mother's face was like looking into a mirror, and seeing herself only older. Oh, how she loved this beautiful woman!....Then she couldn't see her at all because of the flood of moisture in her eyes. It was a good thing that she could instantly feel her mother's arms around her. How warm and comfortable she was.... how tightly she hugged her mother back, and now... Monica knew that she was finally home.

The terrible long narrow highway from Lima to Cusco is one of the most dangerous roads in the world. It changes in elevation from sea level to 11,000 feet. It has so many curves and switchbacks that it generally makes even very healthy passengers nauseas.

One of the oldest Cathedrals in Lima named after the Order of the Franciscan Priests of the Catholic Church

Chapter 2

Present Day – Lima, Peru

In the late afternoon, Lima, Peru was a sprawling hot and muggy colonial metropolis that seemed to stretch forever. Peter Martin was standing in front of the National Museum of Archeology. Earlier in the day he had been to the Cathedral of San Francisco, and he had seen the outside of the beautiful white palace of the great Spanish conquistador and explorer, Francisco Pizarro. The mansion was now the Presidential Palace of Peru. Leaning on the wall for a moment at the entrance door he was contemplating whether or not to go inside. "Why not," he thought, "What else have I got to do?" He'd already been to the Gold Museum and then suffered through the City Tour a few hours before. He still had time to burn because his plane for the Inca Capital, Cusco, didn't leave until 9:00am the next morning. He wasn't a tourist. Why was he down here? He'd really been set up and coerced into this summer job. Peter's graduate professor at the University of California, Berkley, had told him that this little three month internship would help his doctoral dissertation and application to the doctoral committee get passed quickly. But, why was he here, now?....

Peter looked disappointed as the little old man at the front door seemed to take forever examining the small scrap of paper that was his entrance ticket. Was this guy blind or was he just trying to give Peter the full treatment because he was obviously a foreigner with a strange Spanish accent. Peter had grown up in Northern California. His ancestors had possessed their cattle ranch or hacienda for five generations. It had been a gift to his great-great grandfather from the King of Spain, himself, before the Spanish-American war. Everyone in his family spoke both Spanish and English, but only Spanish was allowed to be spoken inside his ancestral home. So, the problem couldn't really be his Spanish, which was flawless, but maybe the stooped old man just distrusted all tourists and visitors to his land. At last, begrudgingly, a knarled boney hand opened the door for him and Peter was through it in a flash, worried that the elderly gentleman might have second thoughts about his admittance.

Really, he had seen all the cathedrals and museums that he wanted to, already today, and it had been enough to last a lifetime. As he wandered down the first aisle, he gazed thoughtlessly, at each exhibit in turn. He at once had his consciousness kick back into reality mode at the sight of a mural of a beautiful Inca princess. All of a sudden he was again feeling sorry for himself. What was he doing in South America of all places when he had just got things worked out with Shelley, his new girlfriend? Peter was determined that this time he wasn't going to mess things up, even though his parents disapproved of her. This one was for real....she was the one. She was his true love, his one and only. He could feel it, and they had only known each other for two months. Wow!!! Had it only been two months ago that she had become his lab assistant? ...

"This Inca Princess looks almost like the pictures of my mother when she was young!" he exclaimed almost out loud. "She's beautiful". The label at the bottom of the portrait announced the name: Princess Lacoya Ines Huayllas Yupanqui, beloved daughter of the 12th Inca King Huayna Capac, and first married to her presumed half brother Prince Atahualpa. Later, she became the wife of Francisco Pizarro, the famous Governor and Conqueror of Peru.

Another wave of melancholy homesickness at once over took him. He could see his own mother in his mind's eye and suddenly he was depressed all over again. He missed his mother's home cooking, and he was upset about being so far away from home. He had never been this far away from home before. "Snap out of it," a voice came yelling into his mind. "You are twenty-five years old for goodness sake and you haven't lived at home except for the summers since you were eighteen years old." "You have to get a grip. You're a licensed geologist working for the University of California. You've got a job to do."

The very next picture was an artist's rendition of the conquistador, Francisco Pizarro, and his younger brothers. Hernando had every bit the size and characteristics of his older brother, Francisco, but he had a gentler and more compassionate demeanor. "Francisco was a lucky man to marry someone as beautiful as the Princess", Peter thought. These handsome Spaniards looked wonderful in their gleaming armor and elegantly trimmed mustaches and beards. Peter was sure that it was really more the artists' conception than how they would have been in real life.

Peter had grown up on the family ranch, the oldest of five children. But, it wasn't beef cattle that interested him. He had learned the family trade and loved to ride horses into the wild foothills of the Sierra Nevadas on their estate. His passion was actually,… rocks. Yes, rocks…. he knew that sounded strange, but even as a young boy he couldn't help but come home from his forays into the hills with his pockets jammed full of all different kinds of rocks. He had loved fossils and brightly colored specimens mostly. Now, as he grew older scientific terms such as ignacious, sedimentary, and metamorphic rocks had replaced the childish descriptions of his youth. His passion for geology had still remained and given him energy to continue his chosen career path even against the wishes of his parents.

Peter continued walking down the aisle and paused in front of a famous mural of Francisco Pizarro and wondered out loud, "What was this man like?" He was a tall thin bearded man with rugged hard features. According to the painting's inscription, Pizarro was born in Spain in about 1471 AD and died in Lima, Peru in July 1541 AD after being betrayed and murdered by his own men. This oil painting was obviously done when Pizarro was an older man, at least fifty years old, and after he had achieved fame and glory. He was the governor of Peru, which at that time encompassed a much larger jurisdiction than now, and included parts of Chile and other surrounding countries. The Peru that Pizarro conquered and the governorship that was granted to him from the Spanish throne was a huge and beautiful part of the world, a "promised land", to some of the conquistadors just waiting to be explored. The conquistadors were all seeking for a magical, golden paradise called, "El Dorado" literally translated to mean "The City of Gold".

This is what intrigued Peter with the whole South American assignment that he had been given; he would be able to explore. He loved exploring. Peter knew that these Andean countries still had some of the richest deposits of precious metals and ores that existed anywhere in the world, and he intended to do some prospecting on his own while he was here. He might as well. His ancestors, for goodness sake, sat on the properties adjacent to the famous gold rush claims in Sacramento, California, for more than a century and didn't even know that they were there. Peter wasn't going to let that happen to the Martin family ever again. The ancestral ranch property took in thousands of acres just south of Sacramento and then up into the foothills of the Sierra Nevadas. Now, of course the ranch was much smaller and many parts had been cut off and sold to supply the needs of the family with cash over the years and generations. The majestic Martin Ranch was still the largest ranch in the area and located just south of El Dorado Hills. The ranch included nut tree orchards, citrus orchards, a vinard, and the cattle ranch. It was actually famous for the old hacienda buildings, and its huge oak and cottonwood trees that had been planted two generations ago. Nobody cared about the little things anymore that made the ranch so beautiful, the only thing that mattered now was the value of the surrounding property. With urban expansion, the value of the ranch was now almost priceless and someday it would all be replaced by houses. The greed for money by certain family members would make it inevitable. There was no real economics to the agricultural endeavors of the family ranch operation, anymore. It was just the loss of a fantastic way of life that future generations would lose, and that Peter would mourn.

Peter returned his gaze to the Pizarro painting trying to focus his attention on the museum's exhibits instead of wallowing in self pity. It wasn't healthy or even helpful to dwell on these family problems. Peter wondered what it would be like to have lived in the time of Francisco Pizarro. He studied the picture more closely....

*Chapter Notes – Chapter Two

Lima, Peru boasts an array of very fine museums. There are both private museums such as the world famous 'Gold Museum' and government owned and operated museums. All are extremely interesting and worthwhile for any tourist visiting Peru.

Statue of Francisco Pizarro the conqueror of the Incas and first governor of Peru

Chapter 3

SPAIN – 1528

The bright green and yellow parrot's feather waved smartly in the breeze as it stuck out of Francisco Pizarro's metal helmet. It had been a gift from his native interpreter, Felipillo, who lived at Tumbes, Peru. Francisco, the adventurer had just returned from a successful exploratory jaunt to the coast of the far-away land known as Peru. He walked briskly up the marble stairs and into the magnificent gothic waiting chamber of the Spanish Court. Francisco was a man with a purpose. He had a dream that was as yet not fulfilled. Pizarro was a brash adventurer who had come back to Spain to seek the help of his Majesty, King Charles V. He needed the funding to be able to recruit and equip more men and ships to be able to return to this land of mystery. Legends had promised that this land would provide the untold wealth and gold that Pizarro was seeking. He also knew that the Spanish throne had a weakness. Spain and the Royal Court had an insatiable need for gold and wealth to fuel its ever increasing operating expenses. These expenses were born of wars with Italy, France, and England. Expenses driven by desires to conquer and expand its holdings especially in the lands of the New World, that the Pope had so generously granted to Spain and Portugal.

It had only taken a few moments to learn from the King's minister that his audience had been cancelled for the day. The king was sick and indisposed. It was yet another setback in a long line of annoying and discouraging days and weeks that were delaying his return to Panama.

Francisco was bored....He sat in the tavern on a weathered wooden chair with splinters that were getting more and more painful by the minute drowning his sorrows in his first glass of cheap wine. The midday sun drenched the darkened room as the large front door of the Inn opened. Several large men flowed through the portal casting long shadows against the far wall. The door closed and the room was again darkly lit. Francisco recognized the leader of the group, Hernando Cortez, an old friend, and second cousin. Cortez had recently returned as well from the Americas in search of more help from the Spanish government. Cortez had become famous overnight because of his exploits in Mexico and conquering the natives in that vast land. Pizarro motioned for Cortez to come and join him at his table. Francisco loved this man. Cortez had been instrumental in helping him get out of debtors prison and introducing him to the Court of Seville. Francisco had been imprisoned for an old debt upon his arrival, before anyone had known of his precious cargo and gifts for the King. These had been specially wrapped and hidden on board his vessel awaiting the time of his hearing with His Majesty.

They were competitors asking the Crown for the same exploration money, but somehow Pizarro knew that learning and developing a bond of friendship with the charismatic Cortez would be nothing but beneficial to him. For the next two hours, Cortez recounted to Pizarro all about his travels, the land of Mexico, and his battle tactics against the aboriginals of the Americas. He explained to Francisco that the natives thought of him as some sort of ancient white god, a long-awaited prophecy of Christ returning to engender the people. They had in fact worshipped him (Cortez) as this legendary god. They believed he was the white bearded man of their traditions that would someday return and save them from all their problems. These native Indians were very superstitious, had never seen canons, or guns of any kind, and were easily frightened and captured. They were all idol worshipers for goodness sakes.

Cortez drilled home the fact that the native cities in these lands were more numerous than the large cities of Europe and that Pizarro's only hope of conquering Peru was to capture the native king, by devious means. He was to enlist the help of warring aboriginal tribes and factions opposed to the Inca King, and thus strengthen his army with friendly natives that could be bribed to help. Cortez encouraged Francisco to train some loyal young men to be interpreters and then establish Christianity among these barbarians and heathens with the help of the priests that would accompany them on their journey. Cortez said, "You must be ruthless, establish law and order through fear, or they will never respect your right to rule. Force them all to become Roman Catholics so that they will be civilized."

One of Cortez's captains interjected, "Destroy their culture by tearing down their temples and palaces and build Catholic Cathedrals over the top of their most sacred buildings. Then you will destroy their will to fight and they will capitulate and become loyal Spanish subjects."

Pizarro returned to his room that night with a fervent resolve to conquer these Inca natives, and bring wealth, fame and honor to his family name. He had a lot to think about. Could he be this strong leader and governor that would not allow any weakness? Could he become ruthless and dynamic just like Cortez?

Two weeks later the Monarchy had made their decision to finance Pizarro's expedition. Francisco had been assigned several Catholic priests and Spanish clerks and officers to accompany him. It was their job to convert the natives and send reports back to Spain once Francisco had conquered Peru. He was given three new Spanish Galleon war ships that could transport 300 men, 75 horses, and the guns and supplies to be able to outfit his small army. Pizarro could choose his own captains from among his own men, but he had to take with him in his command, the King's agents and emissaries to the crown. The King commanded Francisco that he must repay the crown for the expedition expenses from the seizure of Peruvian gold and after the costs of the expedition were recovered then the King wanted a fifth, a minimum of 20% of future gold and treasure. The remainder should be used for the conquest of his new lands and then finally split equally to the rest of his men.

It had taken a whole month to gather a good group of strong young men, equip and load in supplies, and provisions to sail to Panama. Francisco was saddened that he was still short of good, hearty men that he had hoped would join him. However, now that they were two days out and away from Spain, Francisco could finally relax. His three younger brothers, Hernando, Gonzalo, and his half brother Martin de Alcantara, and a young cousin Pedro, were important additions to his army because of their loyalty and enthusiasm. His brothers were already complaining of being sea sick and about the horrid food and living conditions on board, and it had only been two days. They had all wanted to go the minute Francisco announced his intentions to explore Peru. Francisco had originally had doubts about subjecting his brothers to a future of such things as famine, bloodshed, and great danger. Against the wishes and better judgment of his parents, Francisco had capitulated, but now he wondered if he had done the right thing. These young men, however, were exactly what Francisco needed. They would be young, strong, and able bodied fighters coming from the long military line of the Pizarro family. But the reason Francisco brought them along was for their fervent devotion to him, and to watch his back. That was the reason they were part of this company.

Juan, his youngest brother had incessantly begged Francisco to take him along on this epic journey as well, but his mother would need him to provide for the family. Juan was too young and would have to be left behind. It was going to be a grueling trip with no guarantees. Everyone just assumed that they were going to be successful. They had all started out with such wonderful dreams and aspirations. They were very confident that they would all be rich before the year was out. They had really never evaluated the dangers and calculated the risks of this enterprise, but Francisco had.

Francisco looked out across the sea that he loved so much and sighed, "They have no idea what they are getting themselves into or what hunger and privations they will need to endure. Oh, that this journey will turn out well, and that they will once again see their homeland, Spain and their kindred." His vision blurred as his thoughts brought painful tears from his past experiences in the New World…..

*Chapter Notes – Chapter 3

The turning point of the famous career of Francisco Pizarro was undoubtedly when he returned to Spain in 1528 and was able to enlist the help of the Spanish Crown. Francisco was given an endowment of money and a commission that included being named governor over a land that was just a legend and a people that were unknown at the time. Peru was still an unconquered country of mystery and intrigue in 1528.

Scale Model of the famous Spanish Galleons of the 16th Century

Chapter 4

Atlantic Ocean 1530 - Off the coast of Panama

Francisco Pizarro looked proudly at the new wood on the gunwale of his brand new galleon. The wood grain glistening in the sun, wet from the spray off the bow of the ship. King Charles V had generously given Francisco titles and complete authority of the Kingdom of Peru with a financial endowment for the conquest. Pizzaro equipped his expedition with three new Spanish Galleons and enough timber and equipment to construct three more ships when they reached his home port of Panama City. He would be able to carry the cargo overland to Panama City and construct the new vessels on the Pacific Ocean side of the Isthmus of Darien. Pizarro looked out across the vast expanse of sea....It was beautiful. He loved the ocean especially on a day like today. A good stiff breeze, under full sail, and not a cloud in the sky was his idea of the perfect day. And it was rare on this trip. In fact, this was one of the few days that they had not had either rain or storm since they had left Seville. He had spent most of the days and weeks in his cabin planning this new adventure. So, it was good to get out and smell the sea air and bask in the warm sun that was making this day his "perfect day".

Francisco could not help but think of his past voyages and adventures to Panama. It seems that he had grown up on the sea. The leader of most of these expeditions was Balboa himself. Pizarro had grown up in his shadow to eventually become one of Balboa's most trusted captains. Now, it has been nearly seven years since he was executed in the town square of Panama City by the governor…for rebellion. There was sometimes a fine line between loyalty and rebellion to the King. Francisco, the Captain of the Governor's Guard had been assigned to actually arrest Balboa and then later deliver him to the gallows. Now, his friend was gone, and he was the leader of his own expedition, with more men, equipment, and supplies than Balboa had ever dreamed of. He chuckled to himself as he thought about it. "Wow, if Balboa could see him, now!!!" But at once a frown commenced as he quickly remembered that it didn't start out so good for him, either.

"Let's see," Francisco said to himself, "I think the year was 1512 when we landed in Panama at Colon." Pizarro's thoughts melted away like the tide on this beautiful afternoon…. It was a hard land….new wilderness really. The area around Colon was really wet marsh land full of insects, poisonous snakes, and other highly undesirable vermin. Panama was really just jungle. But the new port that Balboa had established was excellent with a deep harbor protected from the surf and ravages of the weather and the sea. Francisco Pizarro was one of Balboa's chief captains. It was a rank that had finally come to him because of his devoted loyalty and brilliant knack for military planning and skill. For nearly a decade Francisco had followed Balboa around the world looking for fame and glory through conquest. But, they had mostly found poverty and hunger and little respect from the Spanish Crown for their many endless privations.

Now, they were finally going to go across the breadth of this Isthmus in search of a western route to the Indies and wealth. They had a very good band of strong men that they had put together. Finally, a group that was worthy to be led into battle. The native aborigines were a small dark, mostly naked people, unskilled in modern warfare, and without armor or suitable weaponry. They had already enlisted the help of friendly natives that were willing to partner with the Spanish in an effort to conquer the ruling tribe of "Indians". They were so-called "Indians" because when Balboa first saw the dark skinned natives he thought that he had finally found the land of India. Balboa had ordered four cannon taken off the two Galleons in the harbor and mounted on wheeled platforms to be drawn by their horses into the wilderness. The difficulty for Pizarro was to establish a trail or road which could support the heavy cannon so that they wouldn't sink out of sight in this swampy terrain. Francisco was so glad to be finally away from the beach head that they had established. They had lost more of their comrades from the sickness and disease that emanated from this swamp than from any confrontation with the natives. Now, they were finally on their way after a month of planning and sending out reconnaissance patrols. Balboa had heard rumors from the natives that there was another ocean across this narrow neck of land and an extremely rich kingdom to the south. Balboa was excited to explore new places and it had also infected Francisco immensely.

The scattered rudimentary dwellings and natives encountered on their westward trek were mostly friendly and posed no threat at all to their conquest. It was on the sixth day of their labored march that the force crested a final ridge. Balboa and Pizarro were amazed to see a huge body of water in the distance. Whiffs of smoke from campfires coming from a large centralized group of crude huts lazily curled up to the tops of the surrounding hills that circled the coastal valley. The breathtaking beautiful sight of the lush tropical valley with a calm blue sea in the background brought a one-word response from Balboa and his captains, "Pacifica", meaning peaceful. That was the year 1513 and Balboa proclaimed himself Governor of this new land and established his capital city. He called it Panama City. From then on Balboa put all the natives he could find to work building his capital city.

An ocean spray wetted the side of Francisco's face and brought him back to the present and his thoughts went fleeing away. The Quartermaster, a huge man with ugly tattoos and several pierced earrings in each ear approached him dragging a young boy. The boy was dirty and wore tattered clothes that smelled of rat urine. "Capitan, I found this stowaway stealing food from the kitchen stores. Should I throw him over the side?"

Francisco caught the squirming lad by the hand and brought him in for a closer examination. With his free hand Francisco had to shield his eyes from the bright sun to get a good look at the boy. An immediate recollection dawned on the countenance of the seasoned Governor. "Juan?...Is that you, Juan? How did you get on the boat….why are you here? Oh no, your mother is going to kill me. Why did you run away from home and come on to the ship?" Juan did not say a word, but just stood in front of Francisco with his eyes riveted to the deck. Now, Francisco was getting angrier by the moment with no response from the young boy. "Juan…Answer me this minute. Why did you do this? Why did you come when you were told to say at home and help your mother?"

In a small tiny voice came the reply. "I am almost fifteen." Then, with defiance in his eyes and with previously unknown courage Juan stood before his older half-brother and with the lion-like voice of a grown man he exclaimed, "I have come to protect you and watch your back!"

"What?...What are you talking about?"

"You told my brothers and me that you needed to have our help on this expedition to protect you and make sure that you have men that you can trust. You go in search of the Golden City, El Dorado. When you find it you said that you will need men who are loyal and can fight. You do not trust some of your own soldiers because they are greedy and only care about getting rich. I will protect you….do not worry!" Francisco's angry expression slowly softened. All Francisco could do was stare at the boy. Francisco knew another boy a long time ago all too well, who ran away from home at the same age to become a soldier of fortune. Slowly he reached out and grabbed him up into his arms and picked him up off the deck and hugged him.

"You shall! My young brother you shall!" Francisco set his younger sibling down again and looked down into his beautiful brown eyes and with a feeling of pride that cannot be explained. "And I shall make you rich for it!" Francisco said with tears streaming down his cheeks. "We shall find El Dorado together!"

The year was now 1530 and Pizarro's last voyage, was indeed successful, and that success is what had prompted the King and his associates to help him resupply and embark once again for the mystical land of Peru. These adventures hadn't always been rewarding. In fact they had been generally the opposite…costly failures. They would soon be in Panama, and Pizarro thought back six years ago to his first exploratory voyage.

Yes, Panama was very different then in 1525. Francisco looked out across the vast ocean, as the evening sun was swallowed up in her wide expanse. The past five years had been a huge blur in his life. He thought back to how Panama City had grown since 1525. It had taken Francisco five long years to get ready with the ships, men, and supplies to be able to return to Peru.

Chapter Notes – Chapter 4

It is a matter of history that Francisco was a lifelong member of Balboa's expeditions. Francisco was also the military leader in Panama City that had to carry out the Governor's order to execute his friend and fellow adventurer, Vasco Nunez de Balboa, for treason against the Crown. Francisco was given a generous endowment from the Spanish Crown, three galleons, supplies, and equipment. Francisco was commissioned to raise an army of a minimum of 200 conquistadors, but he could only find about 150 brave men that would join him on this adventure.

Picture depicting the line drawn in the sand of Pizarro's speech and the '13 Men of Gallo (Rooster Island)' "Who will follow me on to Riches?"

Chapter 5

Panama City -- 1525

Yes, Panama was very different then in 1525. Francisco looked out across the vast ocean, as the evening sun was swallowed up in her wide expanse. The past five years had been a huge blur in his life. He thought back to how Panama City had grown since 1525. It had taken Francisco five long years to get ready to return to Peru with enough ships, men, and supplies to be able realize his quest to conquer this land of mystery.

Early explorers, Balboa, Andagoya and others had been successful in dismantling two Spanish Galleons in Colon and transporting the various pieces and equipment overland to the beautiful new city called Panama City. Francisco's idea to explore the coast line south of Panama gave him energy and drove him relentlessly. Since the new governor, Pedrarias, that the Spanish crown had sent to rule this virgin territory had arrived, there was an uneasy alliance between Francisco Pizarro and the ruling authority. Mainly, the problem was due to the execution of his friend Balboa for treason. At least that is what the governor called it. Now, Francisco was in command of the Spanish army except for the governor's personal body guard in Panama City. Thousands of immigrants were flocking into this Caribbean frontier from Spain seeking to control the land and commerce, and to civilize this new frontier of Panama. Pizarro was given the role of keeping the peace and mostly being a policeman. He found himself longing for exploration and conquest, though. There was nothing here for him anymore. He needed something more, but the governor didn't support his same views. Francisco needed to expand his horizons or surely this current role would be the end of him, a premature death from boredom.

Risking a division with the governor and the Spanish Crown, Francisco determined to complete his quest by explaining to the governor that they needed a Spanish Galleon on the west coast of their land to protect their port city from possible invaders. The authorities reluctantly agreed, bought Andagoya's ships, and now Francisco had achieved his goal. He now had the very means of transport that he needed to explore and investigate the rumors of an incredibly rich southern kingdom ruled from a golden city. He only had to organize the expedition. Tomorrow he would present his plan to his men and ask for volunteers.

The day was the first gloomy rainy day that Francisco could remember here in Panama City. He had assembled his men on the sandy beach next to the newly built wharf. They were in sight of their recently refitted ship, moored just out in the bay. It was ready and waiting. The construction and refitting had been finished only a week ago. They still needed to equip and provision the vessel, but it excited Francisco with how close they were to be on their way to try their luck, and be off on this new adventure. He was sure that it was going to make them all rich and famous beyond anyone's wildest dreams.

It actually took Pizarro two weeks to outfit and lay in all the supplies that they would need on their exploratory journey. He also needed that amount of time to convince the governor that it was a good idea to do this scouting expedition to assess the strength of any enemy forces to the south. Francisco also had to completely assure the governor that he was leaving a sufficient amount of forces to protect their city and man the garrison. The money for the ships and expeditionary force was actually being extended from Judge Espinosa, Father Fernando de Luque, Diego de Almagro, and Francisco himself. Not only were Almagro and Pizarro partners; but, they also shared similar beginnings. They were both found abandoned on cathedral steps as forlorn babies of Castile. Now, fifty years later the two were illiterate cavaliers whose only expertise was really their swordsmanship. They were, however, not short on courage, daring, charisma, and even the ability to lead and inspire men.

For three weeks Francisco followed the coast line sailing against mostly contrary winds in the southward journey. The adverse winds, rough seas, and lack of provisions soon took its toll on the expedition. Almagro was to follow in the smaller, inferior galleon with more supplies and reinforcements as soon as the second ship was ready. At a place with a shallow bay, called Puerto de Hambre (Port of Famine), Pizarro disembarked with his eighty conquistadors in search of provisions to continue on in their quest. Unsuccessful for their search for food, their next landing was at a place soon to be called Pueblo Quemado (Burned Town). Here the unfriendly natives couldn't understand why the Spaniards didn't stay in their own lands, farm, and produce their own food instead of trying to steal someone else's. A battle commenced, Pizarro stood and fought valiantly. Three cavaliers were killed and several wounded in the surprise attack before the Spanish were able to regroup. Francisco led the charge with ferocity amidst a shower of arrows and dart missiles. The Spanish burst forth into the ranks of the naked savages swinging their steel swords like scythes. Even with his quilted mail, Pizzaro received no less than seven wounds, but still continued the assault. The Spanish commander slipped and fell, and several natives jumped to dispatch him. Pizarro sprang to his feet instantly, and with sword and buckler cut a swath through the barbarians. The victory came with a high price. Littered on the ground amongst the dead, two more of their valiant cavaliers were found. The only encouraging news on this day in this despicable place was the large numbers of rudimentary golden necklaces, and other objects that came into the possession of conquistadors. The expedition had lost its charm, most of the cavaliers wanted to return to Panama City. With more intelligence extracted from the natives of their sought for El Dorado to the south, Francisco sailed on to the Island of Pearls and then to Chicama.

Meanwhile, Almagro, moving more rapidly was soon to catch up with Pizarro; but not until Almagro encountered the same unfriendly Indians. In a similar battle, Almagro received a javelin to the face and lost an eye because of the wound. In his rage he set fire to the village and sent the besieged aboriginals into the surrounding wilderness. Pueblo Quemado, (Burned Town) would forever be part of sad memories for Francisco because of his lost friends in their first battle with the heathens. Eventually, the two friends would meet and embrace once more at Chicama before finally returning to Panama City, with their small golden booty.

Panama City 1525

With a new governor in Panama, Don Pedro de los Rios, Pizarro was once again in favor with the governing authority, after months of disfavor. Don Pedro was himself somewhat of an adventuring cavalier. And Francisco found in him a kindred spirit. A new contract was written up and Communion celebrated between the partners, Fernando de Luque, Almagro, and Francisco. Once again they had their two ships provisioned and Pizarro could not help but feel exhilarated with the prospects of finding this new Golden Kingdom. This time the resolute pilot, Bartholomew Ruiz, would bypass the earlier ports of call and keeping further out to sea and would sail more directly to the south. Almagro and Francisco each in his own vessel were soon in a few days at the San Juan River, the southern most point of their last exploration. This season was much more favorable with the sea breezes blowing directly southward. At the mouth of the river Pizarro disembarked at the head of his army of cavaliers and surprised a small village. Pizarro was ecstatic with the considerable booty of golden ornaments taken from the village's dwellings. After a quick leadership council it was decided that Almagro would return immediately to Panama City with the treasure to repay their debts and to again load provisions and get reinforcements. Ruiz would take Pizarro's galleon to explore the coastline further to the south while Francisco would take a group of men inland into the interior and explore the surrounding villages and land area.

After cruising many days the seasoned navigator, Ruiz, was amazed to see an unusual craft approaching them. As it got closer they were astonished to encounter a strange vessel composed of a balsa log raft with a crude sail and manned by natives dressed in elaborate woven clothing and feathered golden headdresses like nothing that the conquistadors had ever seen before. The aboriginal mariners were sumptuously adorned with rich gold and silver ornaments. They were able to understand these native sailors through hand signals and with much difficulty. It was incredulous to the Spanish to view a set of scales on board their raft that the natives used to weigh their precious trade goods and treasure. The beautiful textiles with brightly colored embroidery and trading technology made the Spaniards acknowledge that this was indeed a highly civilized race of people. Ruiz and his men convinced their new found friends to direct them to their home port. Ruiz and his contingent followed them to a beautiful cove and natural harbor that the Spanish eventually would name Tumbes in their newly discovered land of Peru.

Ruiz and his party became the first people from Europe to see the mystical land of Peru from the bow of their ship. Ruiz returned to the San Juan River and retrieved Pizarro's expeditionary force and sailed once again to Tumbes. Francisco anchored his ship in the bay and at once disembarked with an exploratory party to investigate this magnificent city. Tumbes had beautiful carved stone buildings, palaces, and temples. They were all richly adorned with gold and silver and a vast quantity of precious stones, emeralds, turquoise, and amber. The Spaniards knew that they had finally found their Eldorado, because Tumbes was truly a City of Gold. The conquistadors were also very much charmed by the beauty of the women of the city of Tumbes. A thriving metropolis of several thousand very friendly citizens impressed Pizarro greatly. Francisco interviewed many of the chiefs and leaders of the people to ascertain intelligence regarding the Peruvian kingdom. He learned that the Inca King, Huayna Capac ruled the empire from his capital high in the Andean mountains in a city called Cusco. Francisco sent parties to explore the arid coast line and adjoining cities. He called the country Peru, because that is how the Indians pronounced the name of the river Biru. The native tribe that inhabited this area was quite friendly and spoke vehemently of their powerful enemies, the Inca, that ruled this huge kingdom. The tribal chief showed Francisco two magnificent golden vases that he wanted to trade for Francisco's steel hatchet. Of course it didn't take long for Pizarro to make the bargain and to enquire if there were anymore of this kind of golden metal objects that they wanted to trade. The natives of Tumbes told the Spaniards continually everywhere they went, of the Inca kingdom located in the golden mountain city of Cusco. The Inca commanded an army of 200,000 warriors and was ruthless. The Inca king exacted a heavy tax from their tribe annually. If they failed to pay the tribute, many hostages would be taken and sacrificed to their god. Pizarro determined that he would return with an army and conquer this new land of Peru in the name of Spain and of course for his own personal gain. Personal fame and glory were now within his grasp. All he needed was a modern army and Peru would be his. He would return with his golden treasure to Spain if he had to and convince the Spanish Monarchy himself to finance such an enterprise. He was sure that they would be as excited as he was about such a venture.

Rooster Island 1526

Francisco's plan was to wait at the desolate Isla de Gallo, (Rooster Island) with some of his men while Ruiz was sent back to Panama City for reinforcements and to find Almagro. The hope was that their combined effort would be enough to conquer the Andes. Months passed and the promised supplies and reinforcements never came. Pizarro and his men nearly perished with hunger and disease. Disgruntled, all that they wanted to do was return to their beloved Panama City.

After the most animated speech Francisco had ever given…He studied the faces of his fellow conquistadors. To his surprise they didn't share his enthusiasm, at all. In fact, their expressions appeared gloomier than this wet drizzly raining day. Francisco couldn't believe it, why couldn't they see his vision and believe in his quest with the same fervor that vibrated through every fiber of his body. Why didn't they feel it, too? He needed these men. He looked dejectedly down at the sandy ground beneath him. Suddenly, he drew a line in the sand with the heel of his black leather boot. "Across this line leads to wealth and glory beyond anything you have ever known. On your side of this line is only poverty and death. Who will join me?....

Twelve other faithful souls crossed the sandy line that day with Francisco and would be called immortally the "Thirteen of Gallo" (Rooster Island). These caballeros would become the core of Pizarro's expeditionary force that would eventually conquer the land of Peru. Francisco had left behind in Tumbes two of his men to accustom themselves with the country. They had taken some of the natives with them to Panama to train as interpreters and to convert to Christianity. Pizarro was now confident that with the help of a friendly native army, they could organize a powerful force to conquer this empire. During the fateful meeting with Almagro the two friends would disagree and a riff started that would tear their friendship apart. Francisco desired to press on. Almagro and his men wanted to return to get more reinforcements and arms before a full-scale assault should be launched. Francisco was extremely disappointed; his rendezvous with history would have to wait again another five years. Pizarro was not going to admit defeat; nor give up, and he was not a patient man.

Chapter Notes – Chapter 5

Another important turning point of the conquest of Peru was Francisco's speech on Rooster Island. The half starved men that crossed over that fateful line to fame and glory called the '13 Caballeros of Gallo' (Thirteen Men of Rooster Island) would become immortalized in history.

These men became the core leaders of Francisco Pizarro's expeditionary force that would eventually conquer the Incan kingdom of Peru.

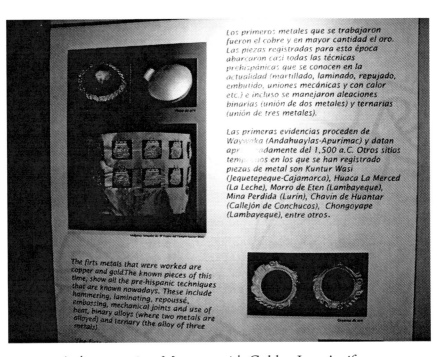

A show case in a Museum with Golden Inca Artifacts

Chapter 6

Present Day Lima, Peru

The history of Peru and the story of Francisco Pizarro intrigued Peter immensely. He went to the next aisle. The display depicted the conquest of Peru with a series of oil paintings. There were also many artifacts on display including an iron hatchet or axe similar to the Spanish military issue that was traded for Pizarro's two finely crafted golden vases. Peter studied the golden replicas closely. "Could there still be such beautiful treasure hidden in Peru today?" That was actually the question that really penetrated his soul. The fine workmanship and intricate detailing done on the gold metal spoke of artisans that were very talented; and also, how the craftsman must have enjoyed an unlimited amount of peaceful time to produce such exquisite and beautiful pieces of art.

What he would give to bring such a beautiful gift back to Shelley in California for an engagement present. His mind wandered back to their time together walking along the rocky coastline of his native Northern California, holding hands as they discovered various treasures among the rocks. Star fish, sea shells of all types and descriptions, beautiful pieces of coral, and all kinds of other treasure were their wealth. It really wasn't about the treasure itself, which was generally worthless to the rest of the world. It was really about the finding. Every time she found some piece of interest, the delight in her little screams of joy and smiles could not be described. Shelley had an unbounded energy and enthusiasm that paralleled his own in the discovery and adventure. She had beautiful golden blond hair that glistened in the sun, and a beautiful figure that could only be displayed properly on the beach in her stunning bathing attire. He knew he had taken advantage of his position as Shelley's boss to make these expeditions to the coast in order to find and categorize some of the local geological specimens. Their relationship had started out harmless enough, but now she was all he could think about. His graduate professor, Clayton Nelson, had warned him of getting involved with lab assistants and cautioned him that it could cause problems with the rest of the students in the classes at the university. Now, he really didn't care. She would have enjoyed so much the sharing and finding small rocks and treasures with him here in Peru as well. Peter had asked the administration for an assistant to accompany him on this summer excursion. To Peter's dismay his request had been rejected. The university was on a tight budget and they were only sending him because of a prior commitment to the Peruvian government and to solidify their position for future possible archeological projects in the country. Peter knew that the request had also been turned down because of his professor's disapproval of the lab assistant situation. Now, it had been over a week since Peter had seen her. Shelley could not come to the airport to see him off because the semester was over and she had gone back home to Southern Nevada to work for the summer. Peter looked down at the brightly painted ceramic tile floor. "That's all BULL CRAP...They all want to ruin us." He muttered out loud. It was a favorite expression that he had learned from his own father during his youthful days at the ranch. First it was his parents and then his professor. When he suggested to Shelley that she come to visit for a couple of days before leaving for South America, then her parents didn't think that was such a good idea, either. So, that is how they left it, with only a promise to pick things back up when he returned.

His job didn't require a lab assistant anyway. The contract was mainly to acquire soil and rock samples, do compaction studies, and to calculate other physical properties of the rock before excavation could commence. This liaison work would be with a Spanish consortium that was going to conduct a hi-tech geological study in Cusco. It was a Ground Penetrating Radar study that could map the underground soil and rock structure up to a depth of fifteen meters using new special aerial radar equipment. It was really cutting edge technology and Peter was actually excited to be part of it. Usually their university was "Old School" as far as the science and technology end of things was concerned. So, this was a bit refreshing and a break from the normal mode of operation to even be involved in such a project. The University was right, they didn't need Shelley down here, but Peter did…

It was too painful thinking about Shelley anymore. He hit his fist to his forehead saying to himself. "You have to focus on the job…not on girls!" With reality again surrounding him in the fluorescent lit building with extremely white plastered walls, Peter pressed on to see other displays in the museum. The first painting in this section was showing the disembarkation of the Spanish Conquistadors at the port city of Tumbes, Peru in 1531. Peter gazed at the pictures intently.

Chapter Notes – Chapter 6

North American universities have had limited interaction with various archeological projects in South American. Generally speaking logistical problems with distance and extra costs related to such programs, unstable governments, visa problems, etc. limit these institutions to Mexico and Central America. There are many deserving projects and only so much exploration money, so most of the concentrated effort in the past has been done where they get the most for the project dollar.

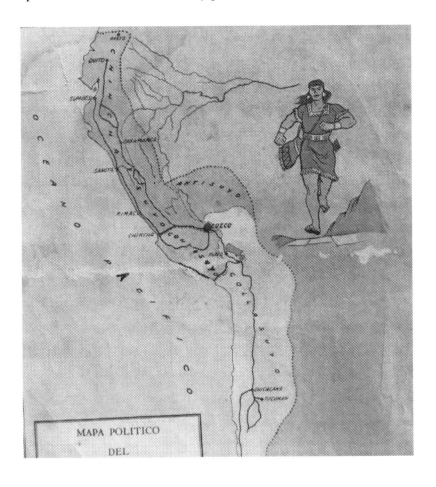

Map of the Ancient Inca Empire of Peru at the time of
Francisco Pizarro

Chapter 7

Tumbes 1531

Francisco Pizarro stood on the shore overlooking the bay of Tumbes. He was supervising the unloading of supplies, and reinforcements. Francisco had established a camp and secured the city. The native citizenry of Tumbes had also provided some token resistance and fought valiantly but were eventually routed. Pizarro was amazed at the difference of this landing and his previous visit. Five years ago the natives hailed him as a returning white God. They were friendly and hospitable, riding their canoes and rafts out into the bay to welcome them. Now, everything had changed. Tumbes was already essentially in ruins and decimated by a rumored civil war amongst the Peruvians. Most of the buildings were destroyed, the remaining people were starving, and the gold and precious things from their beautiful city were all gone.

Francisco had landed two months earlier with his group and marched overland to Tumbes to accumulate his native army of tribesmen. It was extremely easy to form an alliance with these Canari tribal Indians of Peru. They hated the ruling Inca people with a passion, and wanted to join the Spanish. His interpreters, especially one young fellow Felipillo, were devoted to the priests that were teaching them Spanish. The native interpreters were invaluable in finding the information that Francisco needed to formulate his plans for conquest. Pizarro had returned to Peru. This time he had come in force. Francisco had the four mobile cannon brought from Panama City plus over 50 blunderbuss guns. The guns were not accurate at long range, but would be extremely effective in the close hand to hand battles with the native Inca. Also, on this campaign Pizarro had managed to land with 70 cavalry and 220 infantry. He hoped to train and equip another 600 native Canari tribal men to accompany his army, all greatly equipped with heavy arms and armor. Francisco had anticipated the added help and had brought along extra swords, spears, lances, and archery equipment. This would be a formidable modern army, the best that Spain had ever sponsored in the Southern Americas, and he was their leader. Francisco still did not underestimate the opposition, and he knew full well that he would be completely outnumbered. The Inca King, Huscar, was rumored to command at least 200,000 warriors. Francisco's plan really had nothing to do with numbers, but everything to do with surprise and intrigue.

A few days ago, Pizarro devised a plan to prepare his troops for their upcoming campaign. The Island of Puna had previously been populated by a fierce barbaric tribe that was very unfriendly toward the Spanish. Francisco did not want a formidable tribe to control the bay from their island into the port of Tumbes, so he wanted to eliminate this threat. It was also going to be a good practice battle for Tumbes and then the Inca capital. Pizarro ordered his Galleons to open fire on the island's main village. Five rounds of volleys from the Spanish Galleons had rendered the village completely destroyed. Pizarro ordered their four mobile cannon taken off the two Galleons and to the shore.

The heavy cannon were drawn onto the sandy shore by strong horses, but still sunk deep into the soft sand on the beach. Pizarro and his men laid wooden planks under the cannon's wheels and still it was very slow going. The conquistadors had to build a road as they traveled once they got on firmer ground. Francisco was glad to be finally away from the beach head that they had established. Francisco Pizarro had insisted that they have all seventy of their mounted cavalry and most of the two hundred infantry troop of lancers and swordsman deployed. It was the largest Spanish army ever assembled in this new land, and he was commanding the cavalry troop personally. It was the best expeditionary force he had ever commanded and he was very proud of their shinny armor, long lances, and strong horses.

A large group of crude huts and campfires were an indication of where the aborigines had banded together to concentrate their final effort. Pizarro determined to make camp and plan the next morning's battle. Francisco wanted to try a complete surprise attack using the cannon perched on top of the ridge. He would secret his cavalry into the jungle canopy in three different platoons. At the last volley of cannon fire, his cavalry would charge at once with the infantry attacking as well in one body. They were instructed to take no male prisoners, saving only women and children alive. The attack was to commence early in the morning as soon as all the preparations had been made, and the cavalry could be readied in their positions. Now, rest and food for his men was all that Pizarro could think about. It would be critical for their success, tomorrow.

The day was beautiful, warm, and sunny. Francisco was leading the platoon of cavalry in the middle of the assault. The cannon fire commenced raining hot fire down upon the unsuspecting population.

The sound was deafening as it reverberated off the hillsides and echoed back into the valley. The four cannons were busy for a full five repeat volleys making the valley a mix of smoke, dust, and burning debris. The panicked aboriginals could be seen from a far running in every direction without any common purpose. At last the guns were left silent. Pizarro gave the signal and with a loud yell, "May God Bless Us". The cavalry charge was on and Pizarro could feel the adrenaline rush enter his body. The big stallion he was riding seemed to sense the same feeling and he jumped to the task. In a whirl of swords, spears, and blood, it was all over within just a few minutes. In the end there were more than two thousand dead men with their bodies crumpled and spread all over the valley floor. Among the dead were numerous women and children victims of the indiscriminate trajectory of cannon fire. The city was theirs. Well, it really wasn't a city at all, and Francisco realized that the memory of this battle or butchery would haunt him the rest of his life.

With the battle of the island of Puna and yesterday's skirmish in Tumbes behind him, Francisco was more at ease. He determined to send out a patrol to spy and gather intelligence on the Inca strongholds. An interpreter, a priest, and three strong men all dressed in native costume, were dispensed immediately. And, Pizarro anxiously awaited their return. From Francisco's previous visit, he had already gleaned a large amount of reconnaissance. He had learned for instance that the two largest cities were Quito to the north and Cusco which was in the interior high in the mountains to the south. Cusco was also the Inca Capital and where the Inca King, Huscar, resided.

Now, Francisco's only concern was to prepare. He kept his men busy and made sure that they had their cargo unloaded and their defenses set up as quickly as possible. The Spanish Conquistadors, were a unique blend of fighting men and tradesman. Everyone was skilled in the art of warfare and they needed to practice their skill constantly. Each man was a skilled sailor and had his individual duties aboard ship. Equally, important was the fact that each man also had skills and duties to perform during their sojourns on land. The tasks varied from sentry duties, cooking, horse tenders, blacksmiths, supply officers, weapons experts, and so on. Francisco took great pride in organizing the troops and ensuring that each accomplished his responsibility to the best of his ability. This modern Spanish army was disciplined, and hardened in warfare. He had not lost a man in battle since Pueblo de Quemada five years ago. And for sure he was planning on minimum losses in this campaign as well. He knew that it would depend on the cannon, surprise, and a ruthless strike to the heart of the Inca Empire. His advantages were the weaknesses of the Inca: superstitious of his cannon fire, the bearded white men returning to fulfill their legends and prophecy, and his superiority in armor and weaponry, and of course his beloved cavalry. Francisco would implement all of these elements in his battle plan for the conquest of Peru. A week had passed before his forward patrol had returned and Pizarro was sitting in council with all his captains listening to the report from the leader of the expedition. "This is great news…. Are you sure? Can it be true that Huayna Capac, the Inca King is dead?" Repeated Francisco.

"And unknown disease with pox sores has overtaken him, sir." Responded the conquistador. Francisco had seen the destruction already in Tumbes among the natives, in the past few days, and the expedition doctor and reported to him that the disease was Small Pox. The Indians had no immunity to this disease, and it was ravishing the population. In Tumbes alone it was estimated that 70% of the city had succumbed to the hated malady. "I fear that we have brought this disease to these unfortunate souls on our last voyage," lamented the Spanish physician. "How could we have brought such great destruction upon this people that we wish to convert to Christianity and befriend?"

Hernando de Soto, a chief captain spoke up, "we must strike immediately, while they are unprepared and in disarray."

"They will chose another king quickly and be ready to give us battle, soon." Spoke up another captain.

"We cannot wait," hissed another.

"Silence!" yelled Francisco, "let him finish his report."

The conquistador spy stood up again and continued, "Thank you, Governor, the news from Quito is that the Prince Atahualpa has already declared war on his brother, Huscar, in Cusco. The civil war has commenced and they have already fought several battles. Atahualpa is marching on Cajamarca as we speak. That is my report."

"Thank you…this is fantastic news. We have landed in the middle of a civil war, my friends and we can use this to our advantage. We must be cautious, and let the Incas exhaust their resources and their armies fighting each other. Now, we conclude this meeting, and rest…We will meet again tomorrow morning. Go… see to your men and we will contemplate what course of action we must take at our next meeting." Francisco was tired, because he had worked feverishly these past few days preparing for their upcoming march. Although the news was very encouraging, Francisco needed rest. He needed to be at his best for tomorrow. He knew that his next step would determine whether he would conquer or die in this foreign land.

Chapter Notes – Chapter 7

Francisco Pizarro had the good fortune of landing in Peru in 1531 in the middle of a tragic civil war that would actually destroy the Incan Empire. The 12th Inca King, Huayna Capac had recently died of the Smallpox. His son, Huascar, reigned in his place from the capital city of Cusco. Another illegitimate son, Prince Atahualpa, contested for the throne from his birthplace of Quito. At the time of the arrival of the Spaniards the whole Empire was at war with each other. Both sons had been taught of their father's dream of a white bearded man returning to their land from the clouds to the billowing sea to bring their people peace and a new world. He had at his control thunder and lightening. This Wiracocha was the same bearded God, Jesus Christ, that legend says visited this people in the Meridian of Time. It is no wonder that the Incans were so easily conquered when Pizarro came in like manner amidst this conflict.

Replicas of Spanish Armor from the
Conquistadors of the 16th Century

Chapter 8

Cajamarca 1532

After many days of marching without stop, Pizarro's army of conquistadors had finally stopped at the outskirts of the Inca city of Cajamarca and established a camp. The terrain had changed dramatically from the arid desert of the rugged coast line to lush farm land and lowland valleys. After many days of climbing the foothills of the distant mountains they had finally reached their objective, Cajamarca. The city was nestled in a green, well-watered valley with many canyons jutting out on the Eastern slopes of the distant mountains. The higher elevations made the temperatures cooler. Pizarro was pleased that it was certainly easier to find water and feed for their horses. The oppressive heat during the laborious march had wearied his men, and had given way to nice cool breezes coming down to them from the Andean Mountains. It was actually quite refreshing and invigorating. The weather in and of itself was enough to elevate the morale of his comrades. The men were ready and eager for whatever was to be their fate.

Pizarro had sent out an emissary, an advance patrol, complete with his most trusted interpreter, Felipillo, and three strong men to contact the Inca Prince, Atahualpa, two weeks previously. Francisco had found out that Atahualpa was currently basing his temporary headquarters at Cajamarca where he was organizing his army for another confrontation against his half-brother, Huascar, in Cusco. They had thus turned the direction of their march to this city in an effort to meet the prince and have their first confrontation with the Inca. The Inca Prince had responded positively to a request for a meeting in the town square, where they would finally meet. Tonight in the cover of darkness, he had assigned Hernando, his brother, a patrol to scout out the city and the central square where they were to meet in two days time.

This was Hernando's first real assignment to lead a patrol by himself. He was really excited because for the first time his older brother had trusted him enough that he had given him charge of this important mission, and he wasn't going to fail him. When Francisco had first told his younger brothers that they could come along on this adventure, Hernando, Juan, and Gonzalo were ecstatic. But, Francisco had quickly brought their celebration to a sudden halt, with a stern facial expression which was followed with this sobering explanation. "You are only going along to watch my back and protect me, and for so doing I will make you rich, when we conquer the Inca. Since, that time Hernando was clued into the seriousness of this escapade and that even though their army appeared to be united, Hernando sensed certain jealacies and problems that worried him. Besides, Hernando even though young, new the dangers of what wealth and power could do to change a man. Hernando knew of the rift between Francisco and his one time friend and partner, Diego de Almagro. Hernando did not like him either nor did he trust him. He knew how devoted Francisco was to this quest and to the Spanish Monarchy that sponsored their conquest. He also knew that some of their men held no such devotion, but were really here just for their own greed and personal gain.

The night was dark with no moon. Hernando and his three men crept across the wall of the city dressed in heavy woolen native dress borrowed from their friends from Tumbes. Hernando was unaccustomed to the soft wool of the strange cameloids, called llamas. It was however, warm and took the chill off the night extremely well. Atahualpa's army was estimated to be at least 30,000 strong. They were encamped on the other side of the city in a sea of tents which made Cajamarca look even larger. However, the city itself was mostly deserted because the citizenry were uneasy about this meeting of foreign powers in their town. It was easy to find the city center because four main streets all converged right together at the square, with what appeared to be the most important buildings all located at the center and along these important intersects. The streets were paved with rough stones not unlike the cobblestone streets of Madrid or Seville. The buildings here seemed to be made mostly of stone with wood and thatched roofs. The residences were small and quite modest compared to the more important central buildings. There were nobody on the streets late at night, and they had only seen two sentries close to the perimeter or low wall of the city. The sentries were easily avoided and the patrol never encountered any other people or animals for that matter right to the center of the city. There were small lamp lights in many of the larger buildings and the patrol members could peer inside to try and see anything of note in the darkness. The city square was huge compared to those in Spain, and was obviously used for ceremonial purposes and the cultural festivals of this civilized people. Hernando and his men were impressed. This was not the same type of city as the tribal towns and villages that they had encountered in Peru thus far. This was an incredibly well advanced society with an obvious ability to build and work together that was in evidence all around them. It was quite impressive. They stopped to the side of a large building, a palace, by any description with many torches that lighted the outside. Hernando motioned for his companions to stay secluded while he continued on. Hernando tried to stay in the shadows as he entered a hallway that led into an inner courtyard. He had seen something similar in Spain, but it had been owned by an extremely rich nobleman. He noticed movement, and stopped immediately and knelt down. The most beautiful young woman that Hernando had ever seen approached from the other side of the courtyard carrying a vessel in her arms. Through the torchlight he could see how nicely colored was her woven dress that accented her beauty. She stooped in the center at the well to draw water and fill her golden metal vase, and soon she turned and was gone.

Hernando had drawn a map of the city square and the important buildings labeling the streets and anything of importance. He was explaining to Francisco and their war council captains that if they placed their cannon strategically at the square opening of the two streets from the east and west. Then, they would have the sun behind them and if they forced Atahualpa to bring his warrior guard into the other side of the square, then they could concentrate the cannon on them in one group. Hernando also proposed to have their infantry secreted behind the cannon where they could rush the enemy from a united front. Francisco exclaimed enthusiastically, "This is excellent…And we need to divide up the cavalry in four patrols back in the streets that lead to the square. At the sound of the cannon they will converge on the square."

The Dominican Priest, Vicente de Valverde, said dryly, "I thought we were going to convert these people to Christianity and civilize them not destroy them." "Okay," said Francisco Pizarro, "we will let you approach the Prince and see if he would like to hear your message. We will give you the opportunity to entreat him, but the first sign of danger and we will have to make sure that we have captured the Inca Prince and secured the city. Tomorrow at noon is our meeting with the Inca Prince, make sure everything is ready. Make sure that every man is in his place and that everyone knows his duty."

Finally, a bright sunny day and Francisco had been up since dawn. Pizarro had arrived in Cajamarca with 63 horseman and 200 infantry. He had sent his cannon into the city square early and was now marching in front of the infantry riding his favorite black. He had had his personal sword bearer shining and preparing his armor and his horse saddlery for this important meeting for two days now. He was impressed at how brilliantly the armor shone in the sun. His top captain he had placed in charge of the cavalry and cautioned him to hold back in camp until the last moment before the meeting, so as not to alarm the Inca. This was really going to be all about surprise and he would only get one chance and everything needed to go perfect to ensure success.

The sun was high in the center of the sky, everything was in readiness. Pizarro had felt this same surge of adrenaline consume his body before. He knew that this was going to be a defining moment in his life. The Inca Prince's warriors had filed into the square and lined up on the opposite side perfectly as they had hoped a full hour ago. To the Spaniards surprise none of the Inca's army came prepared with any weapons at all. Finally, the Prince's honor guard and procession appeared from the West entrance near the palace. Brilliantly colored feathers and wonderfully colorful tunics adorned the Prince's guard. The Royal litter was magnificent....held up smartly on the shoulders of six strong bearers completely covered from head to foot with blue and yellow feathers, and gold bracelets and necklaces that sparkled in the daylight blinding the Spaniards.

The veiled litter came to a stop in front of Francisco and his leadership entourage. Francisco nodded to the Catholic priest and the Friar approached the litter with their interpreters. Valverde started into a long discussion on the fundamentals of Christianity, stopping at intervals to let the interpreter race in and catch up. The veil parted and the interpreter spoke enthusiastically, "The priest would like to present you with this book that carries the word of God." Atahualpa curiously reached out and took the Bible with his hand and placed it to his ear. After a few moments a frown appeared on his countenance and he retorted, "I can not hear anything". The prince then immediately threw the book to the ground. The priest stepped back, with an astonished look on his face. He could not believe his eyes as he beheld the sacred book in the dust on the stone street. He stooped to pick it up....

Francisco Pizarro lifted his arm and let it fall. He yelled, "Saint James" at the top of his lungs. The signal had been given. Immediately the cannon fired in unison. The blunderbuss of Pizarro's guard cut down the liter bearers and the liter crashed to the earth, casting out Atahualpa, and sending him sprawling onto the street. Francisco rushed to the litter and took hold of the prince by the arm to secure his prize and his long-awaited fortune. Again the cannon fired into the square. The infantry charged into the melee. Horses and cavalry appeared from the four quarters cutting off the retreat with sword and spear of the frightened Inca warriors as they fled in panic. Within minutes it was all over...thousands of Peruvians lay dead and scattered over the entirety of the city square. Blood ran freely into the streets and stained the ground.

A quiet peace again pervaded the air with only the lingering smell of gunpowder and sulfur to mar the senses.

Pizarro marched the Inca Prince under heavy guard to his own palace, and spent the rest of the day securing first the palace, city square, and finally the city itself. Francisco ordered his camp to be relocated into the city with his headquarters to be set up in the palace itself. The huge Inca camp and army had completely disappeared. Francisco was ecstatic, he had done the impossible, but he wanted to be sure that there would be no counterattack and that he could hold and maintain the city. To his surprise the Spanish had only received two casualties with minor wounds that the physicians were now treating. Details were sent out to follow the warriors who had escaped and other details to bury the dead, secure provisions, to plunder and secure as much treasure as possible quickly before it could be hid, and investigate the city itself.

Chapter Notes – Chapter 8

On November 15th 1532 Francisco Pizarro captured the Inca Prince, Atahualpa, in the Battle of Cajamarca. It would prove to be the defining moment in the conquest of Peru. With the Inca prince in custody, essentially Francisco controlled his own destiny. Thousands of unarmed Peruvians were butchered in the Cajamarca Square that day under a supposed promise of a peaceful confrontation between leaders of the Old and New Worlds. Cajamarca was the place where Francisco forever wrote his name in the history of the world, and the history of Peru.

The most prized fur of the Peruvian Cameloids was the Vicuna which was a wild species that had to be hunted in the wilderness areas. It was never truly domesticated as was the Llama and Alpaca.

Chapter 9

Spanish Controlled Cajamarca - 1532

It had been two full days now since the massacre in the city square. The dead had been buried. Prince Atahualpa was now a prisoner in his own castle under house arrest, but was allowed access to his several wives and family. He still remained under strict heavy guard by the Spanish. The Franciscan friars, native interpreters, and Pizarro himself, had all had meetings with the prince. These conferences were all designed to extract intelligence from the Inca so that Francisco Pizarro could plan his next course of action. In frustration with the progress that had been achieved, Francisco had left the Inca's quarters in a huff and placed his brother, Hernando, in charge of the detail of conquistadors that guarded the prince and his household. Francisco had more important matters to attend to and a conquest to manage. It was apparent that the Inca prince did not want to readily cooperate with the Spanish, and their communication problems became acute. It was not easy to truly cross the language barrier between cultures, even with the interpreters. These native Canari Indians who served as interpreters, Felillipo and his clan, hated the Inca. The problem was that they spoke Aymayra, not Quechua, the Inca language. The other problem was that they did not have a very good grasp on the Spanish language, yet either. So, all in all it was not an easy task to communicate with the Inca and to make sure that the translation was correct.

The bottom line that the Spanish proposed was that if the Inca prince capitulated and surrendered the empire, then they would in turn teach them their language and religion and make them citizens of Spain. It was not much of a bargain to Atahualpa. But, the Inca Prince was visually impressed with the Spanish armor, guns, and cannon. Finally, Atahualpa made a proposal of his own. If the conquistadors would release him, then he would pay a ransom tribute of one room full of gold and two rooms filled with silver as high as he could reach on the wall, and he made a mark to signify the level of treasure. The Spanish had already seen their golden jewelry, fantastic textiles and palace treasure that had already mostly been deposited in the common treasure rooms. Hording booty was a criminal act punishable by death, amongst the conquistadors. All treasure great or small was to be brought to the common room to be tallied and then redistributed. Everyone received their own allotted portion at the dispersal. They were all bound by a covenant of honor to contribute all of their spoils and it worked well as long as everyone was true and honorable. However, this offer from Atahualpa was intriguing to Francisco because it was a great opportunity for the Inca people to accumulate their wealth together for the Spanish without Pizarro having to go out in search of it and forcibly extract the treasure from an unwilling citizenry. He, therefore, agreed to such a ransom demand against the advice of his Crown advisors and clerks. Francisco assured Atahualpa that he would be freed when the demand was met. In his heart Francisco knew he could never let his prize captive go free.

It had already been three weeks since the agreement had been made and Hernando had made friends with Atahualpa. Their language barrier had eased somewhat. The Treasure rooms were being filled and there was a great sense of accomplishment amongst the Spanish conquistadors. Francisco had sent out spies and patrols to other parts of the empire and he was especially interested in the capital city of Cusco. There were legends of a golden temple and the Incas referred to their capital as the "Golden City". The Spanish only knew about it from their dreams and they called it 'El Dorado'.

Each day the dark haired beauty that had captivated Hernando the first night in the palace courtyard came into Atahualpa's room to bring him food and drink. Hernando had finally been able to get her name and inquire about her. She was herself an Inca princess named, Lacoya Ines, and she was a gift to Atahualpa from her father the King, Huayna Capac, the Twelfth Inca King. If Atahualpa was in his early thirties, then Lacoya Ines would probably only have been between 18 and 20 years old, at the oldest. She was the most beautiful Incan woman that Hernando had seen since they had landed in Peru, and he was totally enamored with her. She was only a little over five foot tall but was very slender and petite. Her large brown eyes and olive skin were just part of a beautiful picture doll that could only be admired from afar by Hernando. He longed for her, but knew that his brother, Francisco would not approve.

Atahualpa had several wives all of whom took turns visiting the prince and attending to his needs. None of these women could compare to the beauty of Lacoya Ines, the King's own daughter. If Atahualpa noticed that Hernando paid particular attention to his princess wife, he did not show it. So, Hernando got bolder in his interludes towards her with each passing day. He had spoken to her twice in the hallway already with the aid of an interpreter. Hernando had taught the prince how to play games of chance with dice and he was delighted to pass the days with some entertainment. Soon, the prince confided in him and they were well on their way to forging a strong bond of friendship.

It had been two months since the fatal day of the Cajamarca square battle on November 15th 1532. Diego de Almagro had finally arrived with the needed reinforcements and supplies to continue the campaign. The new conquistadors were astonished at the treasure being collected, and they wanted to portion it out immediately. The friendship of the two captains had now turned to hatred. Francisco and his men flatly refused to share the booty because Almagro and his men had delayed their supplies and assistance. They had not been there for the battle and had not done anything to warrant a share. There was truly an uneasy tension between the two groups as the treasure continued to grow daily. The ransom was almost complete and the tallies had been recorded by the Crown's officer.

Francisco Pizarro had Prince Atahualpa brought to stand before him in the prince's own Royal Chamber. It was a stone walled room, decorated with Inca motifs and a large throne or chair with inlaid gold and several layers of llama fur covering the seat. Gold inlaid designs adorned the rear of the chamber. Numerous other tables and chairs were provided for the host of Spanish dignitaries that had gathered for this occasion. Francisco sat himself upon the royal chair and exclaimed. "You have been accused of high treason to the Spanish Crown how do you plead?" The interpreter repeated the governor's statement in Quechua. "Quick man, how do you plead?" was Francisco's annoyed anxious reply. The Inca prince's slow and deliberate response was not helping the mood of the Spanish court. "I don't understand why you are mad at me. What have I done to make your displeasure," was the poor translation. Almagro was now in a rage and exclaimed, "We had your emissaries to Cusco followed by our men. They have discovered your deceit and your tyranny. We know that you were enlisting their help to raise an army to come against us. Your men have killed the Inca King of Cusco, your own brother Huascar, and tried to persuade his warriors to come against us. What do you say to these accusations?" Now, it was Francisco's turn to be angry, "Silence Diego, I am the governor and this is my court." After the interpreter had finished, Atahualpa slowly cleared his suddenly parched throat and deliberately whined, "my warriors are loyal to me and I have pledged my loyalty to you. Huascar would not abandon the empire, so that I could be freed from bondage. They killed him because he is my enemy…." The sound of his voice trailed off into the short echoes of the hallway. There was silence…

Francisco summoned the priests and his captains to surround him for a low murmured meeting. Almagro was even more animated, "Why even deliberate….he is guilty and should be executed immediately." After a series of whispered exchanges with the Spanish clerks, Francisco rose to his feet and walked three paces toward Atahualpa. "By the authority granted to me of King Charles V of Spain as Governor of Peru, I sentence you to death, to be executed for murder and high treason against the Throne of Spain. Again silence pervaded the magnificent Inca palace structure. "The sentence will be carried out on the morrow at midday in the city square. May God have mercy on your soul!"

Hernando's guards dressed in full military attire escorted the prince back to his palace suite using as much pomp and circumstance as they could afford. Hernando hung back and motioned to Francisco that he might have a word in private with the governor. "But Francisco we can't execute a head of state without the written consent of His Majesty! I'll bet if Hernando de Soto and Candia were here, the court would not have ruled against the prince! Almagro is an evil…." Hernando speech was stopped instantly.

"I am the only authority that matters, here!!!" Francisco hissed. "You would do well to remember it, little brother" he said emphatically. "I sense that you have been getting too friendly with the prince and are becoming soft…Remember we are instruments of the King in this land, and sent here to conquer these savages."

"But…But…Francisco, you can't…" stuttered Hernando. "Hush up, my brother," broke in Francisco again in a very annoyed voice.

"I don't want to hear another word on the subject. My word is final. You have a job to do….Go, do it, or I will find someone else to guard the prince and his family." and with that Francisco turned abruptly and strode away. Then, he stopped in mid-stride, and turned toward Hernando and said. "Hernando, it is my wish that you leave tomorrow with the King's portion to San Miguel, our supply depot on the coast. I do not trust Almagro. We will divide up the treasure tonight, and you will also take our portion back with you as well to San Miguel for safe keeping. Then, I want you to go to Pachacamec, another Inca capital on the Southern coast. We must get there before the Inca people have a chance to hide up all of their gold. Get a detail ready immediately to go with you to Pachacamec and to guard the treasure, you may have twenty men."

"Can I say goodbye to Atahualpa and Lacoya Ines?" asked Hernando humbly.

"No….Go now!" came the emphatic reply from Francisco.

Francisco had allowed Atahualpa the opportunity to spend the evening with all of his wives and family together. In the morning it was a touching scene and Francisco couldn't help but have great compassion for the prince. He knew they were doing wrong, but he was powerless to do anything about it. Almagro and all the Spanish court officials had demanded the outcome of this tragedy. The prince's fate had been sealed. Now, this morning the Catholic priests had convinced Atahualpa that if he and his household would convert to Christianity then he would not be burned at the stake, but would be allowed to suffer death instead quickly by strangulation. This would also allow his spirit to go to the next world unimpeded, according to Inca tradition. The prince had asked for Francisco to come to him. "Francisco, where is my friend, Hernando? Some of my wives have asked to join me in death. I would like Hernando to take care of the princess and the rest of my family for me," was the reply from Felipillo, the interpreter.

"He can't," Francisco explained compassionately. "I have already sent him on another important mission back to San Miguel. So, he left this morning."

"Honored enemy….Francisco, I do not trust Almagro!" Atahualpa said in a low voice. Even the interpreter looked astonished. "He hates you with passion, and I fear that one day he will kill you." Francisco looked at the set determination of Atahualpa's jaw.

"I know Atahualpa, but I can handle him. Life is interesting. You know that once he was my dearest friend and now he is my enemy. You know that once you were my dearest enemy and now you are my friend….Fate has an interesting way of changing our lives, doesn't it? Do not worry, Atahualpa, I will take care of your family, and I will take care of Lacoya Ines! She will be well taken care of."

The Prince sighed, and his countenance glowed. "Thank you, oh thank you…she is of royal blood and needs to carry on the royal lineage. You are a good enemy…It is good to have such a fine adversary. My father told me that a white man would come and set up a new kingdom and rule in peace and love. Do not rule my people as I have done, with anger and force, hate and war. Francisco…. learn to love my people and rule them with kindness!"

Those words sunk deep into Francisco's heart, and at once provided a huge knot in his stomach. He was caught in his guile. A few moments ago all he could think of was getting rid of his little brother and the prince so that he could have the beautiful princess for himself. Now, she was being freely given to him, and he was a murderer. Signing the death warrant, and killing a great Inca prince. A gigantic flood of guilt overcame Francisco, and he knew that Atahualpa could see deep into his soul and the tyranny that had transpired, and yet somehow the prince had accepted it all as his fate.

"See to it that they want for nothing. You can do this for your friend….no?" "I will my prince…I will" came Francisco's soft terse answer. .

Chapter Notes – Chapter 9

Historians have said that if two of Francisco's most trusted generals would have been present, Hernando de Soto and Hernando Pizarro, then the execution of the Incan Prince would never have occurred. Diego de Almagro was insistent that Atahualpa had betrayed them, and was worried that his army would come to liberate the prince. Also, there is another theory that Felipillo, the main native interpreter misrepresented and interpreted the prince's words incorrectly on purpose. He was supposedly in love with one of Atahualpa's wives and helped to condemn the prince in order to have the royal wife for himself. Atahualpa was reported to have many wives and as many as 5000 concubines.

The Temple of Koricancha has several beautiful terraced gardens with
fountains of clear running water. Originally the temple garden had
seven fountains and enumerable golden artifacts of animals and plants
that were created by only the best artisans of the kingdom.

Chapter 10

Lima, Peru – Modern Day

It was closing time for the museum. The curator was hustling patrons to the entrance door. Peter Martin looked quickly at the last of the displays on his aisle. He would not get to finish his tour of the museum and decided that someday he would return to this place. He turned toward the door and read the inscription on a display case that had obvious security monitors and wires attached to it. "Golden treasure and artifacts such as these were taken by Pizarro for Prince Atahualpa's ransom," read the label. In bold print a tally of the booty taken from the Cajamarca ransom was tallied to be "5,720 Kg of Gold and 11,000 Kg of Silver" by the King's officers and clerks. This treasure was melted down into ingots by the same Peruvian artisans that made the artifacts under the watchful eye of the Spanish overseers. Twenty percent or the King's fifth of the whole was transported back to Spain in repayment of the Monarchy's original endowment for the conquest of Peru. "That's amazing…" Peter exclaimed out loud.

Peter was waiting at the airport carousel for the last of his bags. He was extremely grateful to see the last duffel bag appear at the far end of the conveyor. He had finally made it to his destination after three days traveling and with all his bags and his person intact. This had to be some sort of a miracle. Peter stepped outside into the brisk mountain air, "so this is Cusco" he thought to himself. A city situated at about 11,000 feet above sea level, "this doesn't look so bad." He hailed a taxi and they were off to the city center.

Cusco was a maze of Spanish Colonial looking adobe brick, two-storey buildings. Usually small businesses lined the streets with living quarters on top or in the rear of each store. The city of Cusco had arranged for an apartment for Peter close to the Plaza del Armas, the main city square. Cusco's Department of Tourism was one of the sponsors of Peter's work project. They were convinced that they could promote an increase in tourism by doing more archeological digs and establishing sites and places of interest that would be saleable to the world wide tourism market. The concept was simple. They wanted to keep people longer in their town viewing local Inca ruins in Cusco instead of other areas when tourists came to see the world famous ruins of Machu Pichu. This way, they would be able to improve drastically their civic economy through tourism. That is where Peter and the Spanish Ground Penetrating Radar (GPR) project came in. They were going to map the underground ancient structures of the actual ancient city of Cusco. It even sounded like fun. "Who doesn't like exploring in underground tunnels?" thought Peter. "This was going to be fun!"

The taxi pulled up to a very normal looking two-storey dwelling. It was one street to the west of Avenida del Sol (Avenue of the Sun), which was a main corridor running north and south through the center of the city. Peter got out, and the taxi cab driver opened the trunk and helped him unload his bags. Peter paid the man, and gave him a friendly hand shake for his help along with a generous tip. It would take a while to get used to the money exchange and using Soles. He was finally here at his destination, this would be home for the next three months.

Most of the buildings in this part of town looked quite similar with red Spanish tile roofs and high white plastered walls, and the occasional shuttered window. Peter knocked on the front door which was only a step or two off from the street itself. After a few moments an old lady appeared in the doorway with a broad smile, excited to see her new guest. The elderly landlady had a round face with pleasant features. She gave him a hug. Peter needed to bend over almost in half to return the hug. She kissed him on one cheek and then on the other. This was more affection than Peter had experienced in weeks. These Cuscanos were a decidedly shorter race of people, and his landlady, Maria, appeared to be barely four foot tall. At just under six foot, Peter had never considered himself tall at home, but here he proudly felt like a giant of a man.

It had only taken Peter an hour to unpack and stow his gear in the small closet and set of drawers in his room. He was already walking to the main city square to do his first day of exploring. The taxi driver had warned him about elevation sickness and cautioned him not to eat too much his first day. He suggested that Peter should get some chicken broth or hot soup which would help acclimatize him. He also told him that eating yogurt would be good to give him some natural local bacteria in case he drank some bad water. He didn't want to get sick the first day in town so Peter had decided to take the advice to heart and stopped at a nearby small convenience store. He bought his yogurt and some small candies that looked good for snacking later.

There were several restaurants that fronted the Plaza de Armas square. Peter picked out one that looked clean and nice on the outside. It had more than the average amount of tables and chairs in the outside eating terrace area. A fair amount of the chairs were occupied by satisfied-looking customers. His decision making process was unclear to him, but Peter just assumed that if the place was more popular, then the food must be very good. He entered the establishment and let his eyes get accustomed to the interior lighting for a moment. There was a long counter with a cash register next to him as he entered. Peter gazed in amazement at the young woman behind the counter. She was simply gorgeous, but where had he seen that face before? "Is the water good to drink, here?" He blurted out. Her inquisitive expression changed to an angry smile. "No, we don't drink water here! Only Coca Cola from America!" she sneered. His second attempt went no better. "May I please have a bowl of soup?" "Look!" she pointed to a sign in the foyer with disgust, "I am not the waitress!" Peter read the writing carved into the elaborate wooden plaque, "Please wait here to be seated." Peter thought briefly about turning around and going out the way he had come in, but the inviting smells and smiles of a pretty young girl approaching him quickly made him change his mind.

Peter finished the tasty hot chicken soup quickly. It had truly been wonderful. He could not believe how hungry he had been. During the process of slurping down the soup, he had glanced at the young woman behind the counter several times. She had been busy doing her paperwork and had never looked up once. She was obviously very absorbed in her work. "Where had he seen that face before? It was familiar somehow." He mused to himself. Suddenly, it dawned on him. "The Princess Lacoya Ines" Peter gasped. "She looks just like the painting of the princess in the museum. "That's amazing." Peter got up and paid his check. He passed

72

by her again and almost decided to start up another conversation, but then thought better of it. Peter was keenly aware of his Latin-American Spanish accent and that she knew he was a visitor to Peru. He saw how intently she was focused on her work. So, he knew it would not go well, and he just strode out into the street to avoid the confrontation.

Two hours later, Peter Martin had visited the main Cathedral, the Franciscan Cathedral, in the square and other lesser buildings. He was totally impressed with the architecture and construction of these early Spanish Colonial buildings from the 16th century. There was gold trim and silver adornments and decorations everywhere. There was even an ornate altar made entirely of pure silver that weighed in excess of a ton. Even more impressive were the evidences of Inca stonework and Inca foundations to the Spanish construction. The hard Andesite rock used by the ancient people would have been very difficult to shape and polish, but it had been done expertly by a society that did not have our modern tools.

Peter read a sign on the government building at one side of the main square that said, "Department of Tourism". He decided to go inside and get some maps and information about the various archeological sites. He had found that it was expensive to bribe his way into places when he could just buy the entrance tickets here, anyway. Usually, the tour guides provided the tickets as part of the city tourist package. Peter wasn't doing things properly, because he had no patience for the structured tours, for sure. He needed to speak to the Department of Tourism personnel sooner or later, so why not get a jump on things, now, instead of doing it on his first day of work which would be Monday.

An older lady greeted him at the reception desk, and asked how she could help him. Peter explained who he was and that he wanted to just look around the city for a few days until he had to start work next week. "You are going to be working with our Deputy Director of Tourism," responded the woman. "I will get her for you, and I am sure she will be able to provide some useful information and tickets for you." "Thanks" was all that Peter could muster before the lady was out of her chair and down the hall looking for the Deputy Director. Peter turned to the side walls of the foyer to examine pictures and posters of Cusco that had obviously been produced for the tourism industry. In his mind he heard the scraping sound of a wooden chair on the tile floor and footsteps. He finished reading a poster on Machu Pichu and turned abruptly into the direct path of the same young woman from the restaurant with the same beautiful face. Peter staggered back, losing his balance and composure momentarily. "It was the gorgeous black-haired beauty from the restaurant!" he thought to himself incredulously. The grin and beautiful white teeth went very well with twin dimples, one in each cheek.

"What are you doing here?" slipped out of Peter's mouth before he had a chance to stop the words. Her expression instantly changed and Peter could see the red rising from her neck upward until it consumed her whole face.

"I work here," she angrily blurted.

"Sorry," apologized Peter. "I am Peter Martin from the University of California here to work on the GPR project."

"You are three days early, Mr. Martin," she said shortly.

"I know, I just wanted to do some looking around first before we got started with the project."

"I am very busy today, I am cannot help you, now. You must come back on Monday and we will talk. Good day!" with that she wheeled around in a huff and walked down the hall. She was taller than he had imagined her to be at the restaurant, maybe 5' 3" or 5'4" depending on how high the heels of her shoes were. Definitely, a mixed blood native Cuscano, he thought. She cannot be of pure Indian blood being that tall and slender.

"Well, that went very well don't you think," Peter said quietly under his breath. He caught the sly grin of the old receptionist out of the corner of his eye and he decided that this would be a good time to make a hasty retreat out of this office.

Peter browsed the tourist markets and viewed the local ware being sold by street vendors. He could not walk down the sidewalks or streets without getting accosted by native salesman showing him their products. It took an hour, but he finally worked his way down the Avenida del Sol until he arrived at the famous Temple of Koricancha, the Inca Temple of the Sun. Peter paid the entrance fee to the Dominican monk and went inside. The Catholic priests had torn down the temple and built a sumptuous chapel on top of its walls in an effort to bring Catholicism to Peru. The monastery known as the Chapel of the Dominicans was built by the priests of the Dominican Order with slave Peruvian labor, overseen by the Spanish Conquistador taskmasters. Hernando Pizarro had received the Temple of the Sun from his brother, the governor, as part of the original dispersal of properties to the conquistadors. Peter viewed the polished stone walls in amazement. He had never seen such exquisite workmanship of stone, especially the hard Andean Andesite. The Andesite was a type of granite, that was plentiful, but extremely hard and difficult to work. This is what he had come to Peru for, he knew it. It was if all his training, education, and love for geology had come together in one brief moment. This was truly incredible. The hour of the day was getting late, and Peter decided that he would have to get special permission to do an exhaustive study of the temple later, and to spend more time, here. Out of the temple garden area Peter sauntered past the fountains and pools of running water. Peter noticed a city museum, recently opened for the tourists. He needed to get back to his boarding room for dinner, but he decided to take a peek anyway. He still had a few minutes. It was a typical small museum, but Peter could tell it was fairly new because it did not have an abundance of artifacts. There were some cases that had nothing in them at all. Peter passed the curator's office walking down the hall to the next room full of exhibits. The door was slightly ajar and he could hear voices. The curator was animatedly speaking in a condescending manner to his associate. The door flew open and clipped the heel of Peter's shoe causing him tumble to the cold tile floor. He jumped up to see the same beautiful girl standing before him, this time with her hand over her mouth in embarrassment. She had been crying and her eyes were red and puffy. "What are **you** doing here?" she demanded in one quick breath. "Are you following me?...stalking me?"

Peter could not believe his ears, "me?....following you? I think it's the other way around," he retorted. With that the Deputy Director of Tourism whirled around and was quickly out of the museum. This time Peter followed after her. He knew if he was going to have to work with this young lady then he had better do some damage repair. "I'm sorry...I'm sorry you just startled me in there. What's the matter? Can I help?"

"No!...Go away...quit following me." By now she was walking briskly away and Peter had to almost run to keep up. They were on the long path that led through the beautiful Temple Garden to the street entrance to Avenida de Sol.

Peter put his hand on her shoulder and turned her around. "Wait!" he said impatiently. He ducked to the side, and a fist full of keys slotted in between each finger of her fist narrowly missed his left cheek. "Whoa! Sister... Hey, what's the big idea I just want to know what's wrong. You know Monday we'll be working together, don't you. Let's start over. Hi! I'm Peter Martin from California,...what's your name?"

She slumped down into a nearby cement park bench. "I'm Monica Rodriguez. This is my first job since graduating from the University of San Marcos last month. My uncle, Carlos, got me this job because he's the Director of Tourism. Nobody thinks I can do the job! Nobody will cooperate with me! They think that I am just a stupid little girl, and they tell me to go away. Nobody believes in me! Nobody! ....Nobody!" she started to sob again. She sat on the bench with her face in her hands crying.

Peter knelt beside her on one knee, "Hey, you didn't ask me. I've been here since 10:30 this morning and in this town of 600,000 people it seems that the only person that I have met since I've been here is, **you**! Every time, I turn around you're there. I believe in you. You've got me convinced!" He stood to take her by the hand and lift her up. She looked up into his face and it wore the most beautiful smile he could ever

77

remember. The smile sent a tingle through Peter that seemed to affect him all the way down to his toes. All of a sudden a cold blunt object was pressed to his back! Two men in black sunglasses with black leather coats were standing next to them. They both wore dirty white straw hats and sneered menacingly.

"Come quietly and you won't get hurt!" the assailant said hoarsely in a Quechuan Indian accent that Peter did not recognize.

Chapter Notes – Chapter 10

The Spanish Chroniclers have carefully recorded that the ransom for Prince Atahualpa included 5,720 Kg of Gold and over 11,000 Kg of Silver. It is one of the largest treasures ever assembled in the history of the world. His famous offer of one room full of gold and two rooms full of silver for his life is legendary. Most of this collection of precious metal artifacts presumably came from his home province of Quito, Ecuador. Cusco was still under the control of his brother, Huascar, during most of his imprisonment by the Spaniards and the riches of Cusco would have been unavailable to him.

The modern city of Cusco, Peru is nestled in a beautiful valley in the top of the Andean Mountains at 11,000 feet above sea level. It is the famed capital of the ancient empire of the Incas. It really dates back to a much earlier time when the city was built by the Chavin Culture at about the time of 580 B.C. Today it is a busy city that has a great deal of its economy based on tourism. Cusco is the center of tourism for the area that extends to the superb ruins of Machu Pichu, and one of the most magnificent places in the world.

The train and its tracks were the target of several terrorist attacks during the 1980's which had a severe impact on the tourist industry in Peru.

Chapter 11

Pisaq, Peru….Present Day

Two hours had passed; the wrist ties and ankle ties were really beginning to be painful. Peter knew he would need to get some circulation going soon or he would lose his extremities forever. He and Monica had been thrown in the back of a van, blind folded, tied up, and whisked through the city and into the country. Peter could sense and feel Monica next to him, and that she was still scared and shaking constantly. "Are you cold?" Peter whispered.

"No" came the reply.

"Well, I don't know about you or Peru for that matter either!" he started. "I told you that I just got in this morning, and I haven't been treated very well at all. I am going to have to report this situation to the Department of Tourism when we get back to the city. I may even have to take my complaint to the U.S. embassy in Lima. Of course, the thing that makes me the most upset and disturbed of all is that I think that I have missed my first supper, and my landlady will not be happy with me at all. She was expecting me at six o'clock sharp for dinner, you know.!"

"Shhhhh…." broke in Monica. "Do you always talk this much?"

Peter could see that his poor attempt at humor had not gone over very well. "Only when I have been kidnapped, tied up, bored to death, oh yea!... and missed supper."

"Shhhhh…" she replied again. "You know that they can hear and understand you, don't you?" she whispered, frantically.

"Well, I really don't care. I was just trying to make you feel better, so that you wouldn't be so scared… Thanks."

The van came to an abrupt stop and the back door of the van was swung open. A thick cloud of dust rolled into the van choking the incapacitated passengers. Then, a smelly small man of middle age jumped into the back and untied their blindfolds. He pulled out a long knife and cut off the plastic wrist ties. A somewhat larger man with a huge pot belly spoke, "get out of the van, and follow us!"

It had been four days since the abduction, and Peter had only caught glimpses of Monica periodically. She had been kept mostly in a nearby mud hut with the rest of the women. These seedy women were obviously attached to some of the men and did the cooking for the group. This mountain hideout consisted of a series of crude adobe mud huts with thatched roofs. There was a water well in the middle of the unkept courtyard. Usually chickens, hogs, and guinea pigs were always running around lose under foot. However, today, it was quite cold and rainy. The courtyard was a gooey mess of mud and standing water puddles and the animals were all hunkered down in their hiding places. Peter couldn't help but be thankful that he was inside and still mostly dry. He wished that he had more than just his woolen sweater, though. He wished that he had his coat that was still back in the apartment along with a set of thermo long john underwear that he had brought to Peru. The short fat man, Hugo, entered the hut and for a full hour interrogated Peter again. This time he asked Peter about his family back in California, and if they had any money. Peter lied, he told them that he did not have much to do with his family any more and that he was just a poor college student at the University of California. He was down here on a summer job for the university. Peter told them to check out his papers and even phone his university for verification. Finally, Hugo went away and lunch was served. It was usually the same everyday, buttered corn, vegetables and some sort of meat that varied from day to day. He was just glad that he had eaten some yogurt and that the water had not affected him adversely, because he was only allowed to go to the bathroom twice a day.

Two more days had passed, and the ground had dried up. It was winter in this part of the world, but that really didn't mean much this close to the equator. Really, the seasons were all about the rainy and the dry seasons. Peter was suddenly glad that it was still in the middle of the dry season. His door opened and Monica was led in. She had a large black bruise high up on her right cheek. Peter wondered what she had said to her captors to encourage such treatment, because the kidnappers had generally been quite nice to him. Hugo, and another man that Peter had never seen before, came into the small one-room hut and sat down beside Monica. Hugo proceeded to again ask many questions. Some of the questions Peter had already answered several times before. Finally, as time went on with no apparent success, the kidnappers went outside to confer together. Because it started to rain again, then they decided to go to another hut, leaving Monica alone with Peter for the first time since their arrival.

Peter reached his arm out closer to Monica until they touched. "Are you okay?" he whispered.

"Yes, but my wrists are sore and bleeding, and I am cold and wet."

"Come closer, and we'll be warmer," Peter said in a low voice. "What do they want with us? Who are they?" questioned Peter.

"They are bad men. They are what you would call in your country, terrorists. They are part of a group that is always trying to rebel against the government, called the 'Shining Path'. They do despicable acts such as blowing up the Machu Pichu train full of tourists, kidnapping important people for ransom, and just plain executions and murder. Whatever, they can get away with that will annoy the government and cause problems with our tourist industry." Monica explained.

"What is it that you said to them to make them angry and have them hit you and beat you up?" asked Peter. "You always like to act pretty tough, don't you?"

"I don't know what you mean. All I did was have a friendly discussion with them. I explained that this wasn't proper behavior by citizens of Peru to enamor foreigners with our beautiful country. I might of poured it on a little thick, because the tall skinny one, named Timoteo, took exception to me calling him unpatriotic, I think. Anyway, he hit me when I wasn't expecting it. They aren't exactly a group of men that respond to the importance of proper behavior and respect to young tourism directors, you know," she moaned as she remembered how much her face hurt. Monica wanted so much to touch it gingerly.

"You should be careful what you say around them. Don't try to rile them up or make them angry and I think we'll live longer," counseled Peter.

"Okay....Okay, but the whole thing irks me greatly," said Monica sadly. I still can't believe these thugs grabbed us. They think that we're going to make them rich!"

"But, why have they kidnapped us?" again questioned Peter. "Well, let's see...Let's analyze this," continued Peter. "I am an American citizen, so I guess that could be a reason. I am a poor college student working on his doctor's degree in geology. No, I don't think that's the reason. I have a beautiful girlfriend back home, but I don't think that they care about that. Let me see what else....My folks own a huge ranch, a Spanish hacienda that's worth millions. I am the oldest grandson and I will inherit the ranch eventually, that is if my parents and grandparents don't disown me first," Peter said with a chuckle. "Hey this is fun. But, I haven't told them about my family, so that can't be the reason, either. So....It must be you they want!!!" He said with a start. "You're the one that they want; they don't even care about me. They could kidnap any wealthy looking American they wanted, and they would have done better than me!" Peter sat up and looked directly into her eyes intently. "So, it's your turn... tell me why they want you? Start at the beginning, please," Peter whispered.

"Okay, but I don't think that I am very important. Why would they want to kidnap me?" she whispered back. "Let's see, ...I told you that I just finished university. My mother owns that restaurant that you visited and I do her books for her during my lunch hour. Those don't sound like very good reasons to me. I am working in the Tourism Department. But why me, why not capture my uncle or the mayor or someone important. So, that can't be the reason, really. If I tell you a secret you can't tell anyone else, okay?...not a living soul. You promise?"

"Sure, what have I got to lose? We might die tomorrow what kind of promise could be that important?" questioned Peter. He was really starting to like this Peruvian beauty with the large dark brown eyes. She wasn't like Shelley at all. Monica was always serious. She never joked or laughed like Shelley. But, she did smile at him in just the right way and it haunted him. She wasn't quite as tall as Shelley, but she had a beautiful slender figure and a mysterious beauty that was intriguing. "Okay...Tell me your secret already. How big can it be?" whispered Peter as he turned to face her. She had a smudge of dirt on the tip of her nose that he hadn't noticed until that moment. Monica was embarrassed, when she realized that Peter had noticed her dirty face. She hadn't been able to clean up and make herself presentable because her hands were tied. "I'll rub the dirt off your nose if you tell me...come on." She turned her face in his arm and shoulder a couple of times to clean her face. It was amazing the tingling sensation that went up and down his spine with her being so close to him, and touching him. It was like hugging without using arms. Peter had to back off, this was not good ...he was off the market by the way. Didn't he remember his girl back home, Shelley anymore?

"My mother is the keeper of the Sacred Quipu!!!" she blurted out in a quiet voice.

"What?...what kind of secret is that? I don't even know what that means." Peter said with an annoyed voice.

So, Monica started explaining, "The Sacred Quipu has been handed down by my ancestors for centuries since the first Inca King, Manco Capac. My mother is last of her generation to receive it. Since, my father and brother died in a car accident. I am the last surviving person in our ancestral line. My mother has secretly been teaching me about it. She will hand it down to me and my children before she dies. The Quipu is a series of knotted colored strings worn about the neck like a necklace to remember important events, places, and the history of my people. The Inca priests were called the "rememberers" and they were the ones that made the Quipu and passed it down. Each knot on each colored string has a specific event or thing associated with it."

"Wow!..." exclaimed Peter, "now, that is something. But I don't think that is why they want me either when I think about it. Nobody knows about the Sacred Quipu except my mother and me. So, it must be something else."

They both sat in silence for a while, and then Monica turned to Peter with trembling lips, "You won't tell anyone will you?"

"No, I promise you. I won't tell anyone," whispered Peter in her ear. With that she slid her head along his shoulder until it rested in his lap.

"Thanks, Peter, I'm tired... can I sleep on your lap?" And almost immediately the exhausted girl was asleep.

The door opened and they both woke with a start. It was sunny and the rain had stopped. Hugo was at the door. "We have sent our ransom demands to your uncle for one million U.S. dollars, senorita, and another one million dollars to the U.S. government for your ransom as well, American. If we get the money we will let you go free and unharmed. If not we will have to kill you, okay?"

It had now been two weeks since the abduction and still no word. The 'Shinning Path' members were getting restless and more irritable each day. The quality of the food was deteriorating daily as well. There was only one other woman in camp now to cook and take care of them. The others had presumably gone back to their homes and families. The number of guards was fewer. The liberties they gave their captives increased. No longer did they require their arms and legs to be tied during the day, only at night. They were watched closely and guarded cautiously, but allowed the liberty to wander around the camp and talk with each other freely. These were days never to be forgotten for Peter. The friendship that was being forged between Monica and Peter would be strong and lasting, built upon this unusual experience. Peter had not encouraged this relationship, and he still kept his physical distance from her. He told himself that it was just the situation, and being prisoners together, that was causing this bond. Soon they would be free and they would both go back to their normal lives…whatever that was. Peter was actually having a hard time remembering life before the fateful stroll in the Temple Garden. Monica once took his hand and started to squeeze it gently, and Peter had to drop it immediately. It was an awkward moment.

Peter at times was uncertain if he was winning the battle within himself at all. A couple of days ago, Monica had come up to him after dinner and said with a coy little smile, "I think that you are falling in love with me. Aren't you?"

The comment was right out of the blue and just about floored Peter. Trying not to be too flabbergasted, Peter just calmly responded, "Oh, yea....What makes you think that?"

"Well, you just can't keep your eyes off me!" she giggled. Monica had this very annoying way of making Peter feel really uncomfortable sometimes. He knew she was just teasing him. Now, he was self conscious, because he did spend a lot of time just staring at her. Monica was getting more and more pleasure every day out of teasing him.

"Oh, don't worry about that. I'm just trying to watch out for you, and take care of you. I wouldn't want any of these thugs to take another poke at you!" Peter said with a laugh. All that night, though, Peter did wonder if it were true!...Was he falling in love with this Peruvian beauty? Or was she just driving him crazy, with those hypnotic eyes?

On day 22, Hugo, came up the dirt road to the camp in the rusty van. He got out doing some extraordinary animated whooping and hollering. The 'Shinning Path' had been informed that the money had finally been transferred to their off-shore account the day before. Hugo unpacked an ample supply of Chicha, Andean beer, made from corn. The cache was really enough beer for 12 men, not just six. There was much rejoicing all afternoon.

Hugo told Peter and Monica that they would take them to a town in the morning and let them go free at a busy intersection where they could catch a bus. Peter asked them, "why wait? We are just as happy to go to town this afternoon. We would like to go home right away, like you promised." Hugo just stared at him and laughed. At dusk as per usual they were tied up in their own huts. It had only been two or three hours into the night when all sounds of drunkenness had died out. The camp was deathly silent. The fire had died down, and the torches were all gone out. Peter knew that his captives were in a complete drunken stupor. He had found a broken piece of glass two days ago near the well, and he had placed it in his hut where he could use it to cut the bonds at night if they decided to escape. Peter felt uneasy about Hugo's intention to let them go. He did not trust him. Finally, Peter broke the rest of the bonds on his wrists and he feverishly started on the bonds about his ankles with the sharp glass. He crept outside waiting for a few moments before he moved ahead to ensure that everyone was asleep.

The door to Monica's hut squeaked a tiny bit, and he was quickly inside. Peter was lucky. Tonight the cooking woman was with her man in another hut, and not in Monica's cabin. Peter put his hand on her mouth and whispered into her ear softly, "we're leaving!" Those big dark brown eyes fluttered open and she was startled until she recognized him and then she just smiled. Monica kissed his hand and he withdrew it in an instant. A few moments with the piece of glass and the bonds were cut and they ran out into the black starless night. They went slow at first, picking their way in the darkness keeping to the road and making as little noise as possible. As soon as Peter felt they were safe, a few hundred yards away they started running down the mountain side on the rocky road. It had many switchbacks, but in the darkness Peter did not want to wander off the road. Going cross country would be faster, but they couldn't risk the dangers of getting off the road in the dark. They could twist an ankle or fall and break a leg in the brush. So, they just kept running, and running. Finally, Peter, could tell that Monica was exhausted. They slowed to a walk. "Why did we escape if they are taking us home in the morning," asked Monica finally out of breath and coughing.

"I don't trust Hugo…Do you?"

Monica thought about that for a moment, "I guess I don't," she said knowingly.

"I think that they planned to kill us all along, but they kept us alive in case they needed more bait to get the money. Now that they have their money then they don't need us anymore. I think that they planned on killing us anyway so that we couldn't identify them later. We were just going to be a liability to them, now. They were definitely going to kill us."

That thought gave Monica the shivers all over her body. "Let's run some more…Okay?" Monica gasped.

After another mile they had to stop to rest again. Monica caught Peter's arm and leaned on his shoulder. After a few minutes, she panted in between breaths. "And here all this time I thought you didn't want to escape just so you could spend more time with me! I'm so disappointed," Monica giggled as she started to run. "I'll race you to the bottom of the hill!"

Chapter Notes – Chapter 11

The 'Shinning Path' organization still exists in Peru today. It is a collection of terrorists, thieves, and murderers that have the intent of bringing down the government of Peru in favor of the historical ruling party of the native Incan people. During the 1980's the 'Shinning Path' almost effectively curtailed tourism and destroyed the economy of Cusco because of continually blowing up the tourist trains to the Machu Pichu ruins.

Two young Peruvian girls in their native costume with the Temple of Koricancha and the temple garden in the background.

Chapter 12

Cuzco—Present Day

By daybreak Monica and Peter were in the back of an old dilapidated army truck that was taking vegetables into the city's marketplace. Peter thanked the driver and gave him an American twenty that he had hidden in his underclothes for the past three weeks. The kidnappers had taken their wallet and purse, with all of their ID. The terrorists had everything with them, which included their money as well, so Peter was thankful for the hidden twenty dollar bill. They were dropped off at the police station near the Cusco airport. For the next two hours they were again being interrogated and questioned. A ream of paperwork was filled out, and relatives were notified. The military general, General Rojas, in charge of the Cusco area came to the police station and made Monica and Peter show him on the maps where the 'Shinning Path' hideout was, and describe to him all they could remember about the camp. Within the hour, General Rojas had mobilized his forces and two helicopter gunships. Monica was finally taken home. But the general insisted that Peter go with him in one of the gunships to make sure that they had the right camp.

Two armored personnel carriers were in position driving up the narrow mountain road. The kidnappers were not going to be able to escape. They were not very good military minds, having only one escape route in and out of their hideout. By the second fly by with the gunship, Peter was sure that this was the right place. "General, don't you think that we should just arrest them, and then throw them into prison? You aren't going to just kill them are you?" asked Peter incredulously.

"Son, here in Peru against terrorists, we shoot first and ask questions, later. Besides it was you Americans in your movies that taught us to do it this way...don't you know?" The helicopters made their strike run with enough rockets and fire power to destroy a small city. On the next pass, Peter could not see a single tree or bush in the clearing, just smoke. The whole camp was just a dark black charred hole. The huts were gone. The people were gone. The animals were gone. Even the vegetation was gone. Peter felt nauseas, and it wasn't just the low level helicopter flying that was making him sick.

Peter sighed, "That's terrible general, just terrible."...

The general spoke loudly in his headset, "good job men....we'll let the patrols mop up and secure the area. Return to base."

Peter sat at the breakfast table with General Rojas and his officers. He had not eaten a thing. The general laughed good-heartedly. "Your first mission, huh. Well, son, don't let it be your last. We can use good men like you, come by and drop in anytime," the general laughed. "Peter, you will have to leave for the United States immediately, because you are now a security risk for us in Peru."

"General Rojas, I am not done with my research here in Cusco. I need a few weeks to finish my project. Could I just report in to you on a daily basis until I'm done? I would give a good report to my embassy personal if you would let me continue to do my work. Then, I'll be gone, and you won't have to worry about me anymore, general," Peter replied.

The general could see that it might be better politically to have Peter on his side, and to promote good relations between Peru and the U.S. So, the general simply said, "Peter, you drive a hard bargain, but if you do give the U.S. government a good review of the way we have dealt with this situation and don't go to the news media about the abduction or the terrorists, then maybe we can work something out. You must check in daily and also work with our police who will want to keep up a 24 hour surveillance on Monica and you for a while."

"Okay, as long as I can stay for a few weeks to finish what I came here to do. Thank you, general. Thank you." Peter was grateful. He knew that General Rojas was going out on a limb for him. He could very easily have been sent home, with nothing accomplished. The military drove him back to his apartment in an unmarked black sedan. His landlady, Maria, met him at the door and gave him his second hug and it had only been his second time so far in the apartment. All he wanted was a good shower and a warm bed. He was sure that he would be able to sleep for a week.

The central phone office was the only place in Cusco that Peter could place a long distance phone call to Southern Nevada, and pay for it with cash. He had made an appointment ahead of time for 11:00am. That would be 6:00am Pacific Time and he was certain that Shelley would be home and just getting up to get ready for work. He had already written her two emails from his own computer, but Shelley had not responded. He had to talk to her. He missed her so, so much. "Shelley!…Hi, this is Peter! How have you been?"

A gasp came over the phone. "Peter?…Hi, how are you. I haven't heard from you in over a month!" The voice came unclear over the scratchy line.

"Hey, do you still love me? How's my best girl?" beamed Peter. Silence on the line, nothing but silence.

"Oh, Peter….I'm engaged. I'm sorry."

"What!" yelled Peter. "How could you do this? I've been away, and not been able to phone you for a few weeks, and now you're engaged… Why? How?…"

"Oh, Peter…" came the terse response again. "You never called. I was going out of my mind. You were gone for a whole month, so I started going out with my old boyfriend, Jordan. My mother had it all set up even before I got home. I didn't know…I didn't know. And well, your folks don't like me and my folks don't like you…so…it's better this way. Don't you think?"

"But…But…" broke in Peter. "I love you and you love me doesn't that matter?"

"I know…I know…" sighed Shelley. "But, it's better this way….good-bye, Peter," and with that there was an audible click and she was gone.

"Shelley…Shelley….are you there?" There was only silence….and more silence on the phone line, not even a crackle.

"Today is Friday and the Department has given Monica another day off to rest and recuperate. She doesn't have to be back to work until, Monday," said the older lady at the reception desk. Feeling dejected, Peter turned and made his way out.

"Man, I'm not having much luck lately, am I?" Peter said under his breath. "I guess the next move is to contact Balboa Explorations, the Spanish group of engineers and scientists that already have a month's head start on me." He looked down the street and then realized that he had not eaten lunch, yet. He would check out his favorite restaurant in the City Square. Actually, it was the only restaurant that he had eaten at since he had been here in Cusco.

It was the same pretty waitress that met him at the "Please Wait to be Seated" sign…but there was no Monica in sight. Peter ate lunch and then headed back to the apartment. He had two messages, one from Monica and the other from the Spanish consortium, Balboa Explorations. Monica asked him to meet her at their favorite temple garden bench at 5:00pm and Balboa was having another operations meeting at 1:00pm at the conference room in the back of the Koricancha Museum. Peter thought that was odd to have two meetings on the same day, less than one hundred yards apart at roughly the same time. He put it out of his mind. That was fine. It meant less walking and he would be able to do both meetings easily.

The Balboa people questioned him about the kidnapping and all that had happened. Peter liked these Spanish guys. They were all business and were certainly good at their jobs. "We still need to get the permits to do the work on the ground and be able to excavate," said Pablo obviously the leader of the Spanish group. "The girl, Monica, that was kidnapped with you is the Deputy Director of Tourism. It was her job to get the permissions done two months ago and its holding us up." He again emphasized his annoyance with her incompetence. "We cannot do a lot more until we get the city, Department of Tourism, and the Catholic Church all talking to each other." Thanks everyone, I just want to stay a little longer with Peter and bring him up to speed on what we've accomplished already. Thanks…"

Over the next hour Pablo and Peter sat alone going over the project operation and their progress. "This is truly remarkable…I can't believe it….It's just incredible!" exclaimed Peter.

Pablo laid out a large map of Cusco on the table. There was a line that was drawn from North to South and another that went East to West. At the intersection of those lines was the Plaza de Armas. The North – South trajectory went down the Avenida del Sol (Avenue of the Sun) from south of the Temple of the Sun (Koricancha) to the north clear to the top of the hill and the Fortress of Sacsahuaman. Along the lines on the map were dots of all the major Inca palaces, temples, and important buildings. The lines of course were the Ground Penetrating Radar (GPR) projections that had discovered the underground tunnels from five to fifteen meters in depth that connected all the ancient Inca sites. "The Spanish conquistadors enforced the Catholic Priests wishes to tear down the old Inca Culture and built on top of the old foundations a 'New World', thus started the Inquisition period of Peruvian history. The poor Peruvian peasants were forced into servitude and became the strong backs that the Conquistadors depended on to construct their new colonial civilization. Cusco has more cathedrals and churches than any other city in the new world per capita primarily built during the 1500's and 1600's."said Pablo.

"So, all these ancient Inca buildings were connected by these secret passage ways and tunnels?" asked Peter as his eyes surveyed the map intently. "This is just fantastic!"

"Peter we need you to do a study of the rock and soil types in the tunnel areas. We need to know what we are dealing with. We need to know what the tunnels are made of, and how stable they will be if we are able to excavate and enter certain areas. We are ordering special suits and air breathing equipment in anticipation of being able to explore the tunnels. Here are the individual GPR reports on the various areas. You can use them for your study. See you on Monday morning."

"Thanks," was all Peter could manage as they walked out of the museum together. Peter had another hour to kill before his meeting with Monica. While he waited, Peter had an opportunity to view and explore the fountains and the temple garden. Peter could also see the foundation courses of the temple wall itself from the garden. Legends spoke of beautiful golden artifacts that were placed in the temple garden. Corn stalks, animals, birds, insects, all kinds of other artisan works made of solid gold were supposed to have adorned this special place. It was the garden of the Sun. Originally, it was watered by five fountains which flowed pure mountain water from underground stone pipes. Now, only one fountain still remained flowing to provide water to the beautiful stone pools and the garden area itself. The temple garden was truly magnificent even today. With all of the golden artifacts then it would have been spectacular.

Monica was wearing a gorgeous red party dress with white lace around the neck, sleeves and hem of the dress. "You sure look nice tonight. What's the occasion?" Peter said as he greeted her with a wry smile.

"Oh, I was planning to go to a dance tonight put on by the city, but I don't have an escort!" She said with those same dimpled cheeks that had haunted him before.

"You have the advantage on me; I am not dressed for the occasion." responded Peter.

"Who said that I was inviting you?" she said with a little laugh. Peter just looked at her. He could not believe his ears.

"You laughed….You laughed!" he repeated again.

Chapter Notes – Chapter 12

In 2000 a Spanish scientific consortium did do a ground penetrating radar study in which they detailed what they consider to be the famed underground tunnels of the ancient Inca capital. A map of the city of Cusco is provided to show the findings of this important study. The tunnels of Cusco have long been a legendary feature of the capital city of the Inca Empire.

Plaza de Armas is the Main City Square of Cusco Peru

Chapter 13

Cusco, Peru - Modern Day

Monica's pretty red dress swished a bit as she shifted her weight and attempted to rise up from off their bench. Peter instinctively held out his hand to lift her up. His heart leaped within him at her touch as he looked at her smooth elegant hand in his, so small, yet so strong and warm. Peter brought her in close to him. There was a moment when their eyes met. That smile again captivated him, and his face was so close and her lips so inviting, that he thought he might steal a kiss. He quickly turned away….He knew that this time he was blushing. His actions had betrayed his thoughts. If they were to work together he couldn't afford to compromise their friendship. "May I accompany you to the dance my fine lady?" he entwined with a grin.

"Well, now…Thank you….Yes, I would love to go to the dance with you…my fine gentleman…. that is the proper question, and proper invitation for a splendid evening. I thought that there might be a chivalrous bone in your body. A true lady must wait to be asked and not be doing the asking. Thank you…"

"May I call us a cab, my beautiful senorita?" He smiled at her. "First, we'll go by my apartment so I may change and then you can direct us to the ball." He said still mocking a gentleman's pander. "Why did you choose me? Surely a cute girl like you has many boyfriends that call upon you? You could probably have your choice of any guy?" questioned Peter in a bit of a mocking tone. The smile turned to a bit of a straight face and then that frown that he didn't like very much. And all of a sudden, Peter was sorry that be had pushed his luck, and he knew he had said too much.

"Well, I do need to talk some business to you this weekend, before work on Monday." She said carefully. Monica was having lots of fun showing Peter some of the local Peruvian dances during the evening. Peter was really a fast learner and a fairly nimble dancer. He kept apologizing for his incompetence on the dance floor. But actually, Monica had been quite impressed with Peter's willingness to show her a good time and meet all of her friends. Peter was really quite the gentleman, and not a bad dancer in her mind, either. "Peter, let's go outside for some fresh air. I need to tell you something," she whispered. Peter smiled at her, and took her by the hand again. He was generally getting used to holding her hand tonight. It still excited him every time he did it, though. The City Hall building where the ball was being held was the same building that was used as Pizarro's palace or governor's mansion in Cusco. It had the original stone foundations of the great Inca Palace. City Hall was fronted by the Plaza de Armas, the main city square of Cusco. They walked hand in hand into the beautiful square all lit up on this special evening. It was too dark to fully appreciate the beauty of the flowers and shrubbery, but Peter could certainly smell their fragrance in the pleasant evening. He wasn't sure if it all emanated from the flowers or maybe some of the fragrance came from Monica. Anyway, she was sure confusing him a lot lately. "Peter, I don't know what to do anymore to get the permissions that we need from the Catholic Church and the Priests," she said seriously. "I have approached them several times and they won't even talk about it. They don't want to have anything to do with us." Peter could see her sad face in the lamplight of the square.

"But, Monica, don't they know how important this is to us, and how important it is to the government that we do this project? It will be fantastic for tourism and for the economy of Cusco and all of Peru," said Peter with an exasperated look.

"Peter, I don't know what to do..." she started to cry. "Everyone is depending on me, and I am going to fail them. I'm going to get fired." She continued to sob.

"Now... Now...Don't worry...I will help you...We'll work on this together. We'll figure something out...I promise you."

"Oh, thanks.... Peter, you'd do that for me?" She sniffled into a handkerchief. They were silent as they walked past a man leaning up against a lamp post. It was early evening, but the main square appeared to be almost deserted. Peter squeezed her hand.

"Yea, sure, I'd do anything for you. Don't you know?" Before Peter knew it, a dark handle with a long knife blade shimmered in the light and was instantly against her neck.

"What the...Who are...?" Peter stammered.

"Shut up!…Don't say a word…Walk!….straight ahead," rasped the assailant.

"Hugo?…." Peter gasped…he had recognized the voice. "How did you escape?" asked Peter.

" Shhhh …didn't I tell you to be quiet." He said with a menacing whisper. "I was up early in the morning going to the privy out of the camp when I heard the helicopters and before I could warn the others, my hideout was blown to smithereens. I'm going to kill you for it…You killed all of my friends…They're all gone! I'm now going to kill the both of you," he sneered.

"Let her go, Hugo," Peter demanded. "I'm the one you want." Hugo turned to look at Peter with an evil sneer, just in time to get Peter's fist in the face. Hugo dropped the knife and staggered back a step. Two shots rang out in the night and echoed off the buildings around the square. Hugo seemed to instantly rise up off his feet and was blown back a couple yards and lay silent in an awkward position on the cobblestone path. People came running from every direction. Moments ago the square was all but deserted, and now a large group of people gathered around them. Peter just stood there stunned. Monica was completely hysterical and crying uncontrollably. Peter caught her up into his arms, and held her close. He whispered, "Monica are you alright?" Two plain clothed policemen were surveying the body. They took control and dispersed the gathering crowd.

"You're lucky! Your uncle was so concerned about your safety that he made sure that we were assigned to watch out for you and your safety twenty four-seven." The officer commented dryly.

Monica started to cry even louder and Peter held her even tighter. "Well, I guess we've had enough excitement for one night."

"We will need you to make a statement down at the police station, Mr. Martin," said the other officer.

"How about in the morning," Peter said wearily. The officer nodded sympathetically. "And now…Why don't I walk you home, my lady?" He soothed as his embraced loosened and he took her hand in his.

Peter was seated in the reception area of the Department of Tourism as soon as the doors opened at 9:00am on Monday morning. He did not have long to wait. In a few moments the door opened and Monica entered the room dressed in nice business suit attire. She grinned at him. "Are you ready?" she asked. She acted as if nothing had happened the other evening. Peter didn't want to ask if she were okay or remind her in anyway of that unforgettable night. They spent the next three hours entreating, explaining, and more or less begging for cooperation with the various ecclesiastical leaders of the Catholic cathedrals and chapels that were involved in the Cusco study. The answer was the same at each location and with each group of priests. Not just a simple 'no', it was always an emphatic 'No'. In fact they did not want to participate at all in the project. It had been a very disappointing morning.

"Come on," Peter motioned, "I will buy you lunch. In fact I know where they have the best soup and sandwiches in town." At the 'Inca House' the Rodriguez's restaurant, Peter was sitting at his favorite table. He was seated across from Monica admiring the house menu. "Wow, you guys have a great place, here," said Peter. "Yea, it's been in our family for generations," said Monica proudly. "Actually, it was part of Francisco Pizarro's own assets given out in the dispersal of properties to the conquistadors in 1538 when Pizarro was the first governor. Francisco was my great great great great-grandfather and his wife was the Inca princess, Lacoya Ines. I shouldn't really be telling you this. I don't know why I told you …" Monica's voice trailed off softly.

"Well, it's a beautifully elegant building and restaurant," smiled Peter.

"Thanks…." Her face was red and she was embarrassed. A nice looking middle-aged lady approached their table and Peter stood. He would know Monica's mother anywhere. Eva Rodriquez was just an older version of her younger beautiful daughter. Monica kissed her mother first on one cheek and then the other. Then she turned to look at Peter. "Mother, this is my friend, Peter. He is the young American that I told you about."

"I'm pleased to meet you, finally. You have now saved my daughter's life, twice. May I join you for lunch?" smiled Eva Rodriguez.

"Sure…" was all Peter could say.

For an hour over lunch they had a great time, laughing and getting acquainted. All too soon Monica and Peter had to leave for a meeting with the Spaniards. Monica stood…"Peter we must go. We're going to be late." Peter stood as well and was about to shake hands good-bye when to his surprise Mrs. Rodriguez took him into her arms and gave him a warm Peruvian hug that lasted longer that he expected, and of course the standard kiss on either cheek.

Embarrassed he stepped back a little and she smiled and said, "thanks, Peter."

"Sure…no problem," said Peter with a quiet voice.

In the board room in the back of the Temple of Koricancha museum the meeting with Pablo and the rest of the group of the Balboa Explorations did not go very well. "We are very disappointed," was Pablo's response.

"What should we do now?" was another's question.

"I don't know," offered Peter. "I need to stay here for a few more weeks to finish my part of the study."

"Unless, the mayor or the Peruvian government can somehow force them into cooperating then I'm afraid that we will not get the excavation permits that we need," sighed Monica. "The civic government does not want the streets dug up, either. Most officials that we've talked to that have seen the maps believe that the tunnels that you are picking up in the GPR study are just the underground sewage system and the ancient water canals."

"We know that they are different systems, and we know that these tunnels are the real ancient tunnels built by the Incas. But, the only way to really be certain is to enter and explore them. Okay…well, go ahead and continue to work on it. We are returning to Spain, then. We've been away from our families for two months already, and we will stay in touch with you. I need to talk to our company president and board of directors about all of this before they pull our funding, anyway," lamented Pablo.

Again Peter and Monica found themselves sitting alone on the stone bench in the beautiful Temple Garden. The meeting had been very depressing. Monica was dejected and very disappointed, so Peter decided he needed to try and change the subject and lift her spirits. "You know something, Monica?" Peter started. "I already knew who you were the first time I laid eyes on you!"

"What!" exclaimed Monica. "What do you mean? What are you talking about?"

"I saw a picture of you in Lima, in the National Museum of Archeology. It was an oil painting of the Inca Princess, Lacoya Ines. You look exactly like her...only in a business suit," he grinned.

"Wow..." Monica said, "Really?"

"Yep, I think all the women in your family are gorgeous, especially the smile with the dimples." Peter said partially teasing.

"Okay, I can tell you really like my mother," she giggled. "But, isn't she a little old for you?" Monica teased. Peter went red in the face. "What about that girlfriend of yours?"

Peter looked away. He slowly got up and said, "I guess I better get back to the apartment. My landlady will be asking me again why I never show up for supper." And with that, Peter was quickly walking back to the Avenida del Sol (Avenue of the Sun) and off to his apartment retreat.

The last thing Peter wanted was to complicate his life. He surely didn't want to admit that he had fallen for this beautiful dark haired beauty, 7000 miles from home. He didn't love her anyway. They were just friends. "Sometimes, if you are placed in unusual stressful circumstances with someone, then your emotions could play tricks on you; couldn't they?" He thought to himself. He didn't want to think about it anymore. He had a job to do. He needed to finish it quickly, and he could be out of here, soon. It looked like they would be shutting this project down early, anyway. 'California', the word never sounded so good, before.

He would make a study of the Koricancha Temple, the buildings on the tunnel map, and of the Sacsahuaman fortress. He would maybe take some soil and rock samples and package them up to send back to his lab at the university. Let's see, he still wanted to have a look around the countryside for evidences of mineral deposits. Peter did a quick calculation in his head. I could have this thing wrapped up in three weeks to a month. "Wow!...I could be home a month early," he said to himself, musing thoughtfully. "No problem. I will have plenty of time to win Shelley back before the wedding. Besides, she is still planning to be my lab assistant for one more semester at the university. I can do it. I know she still loves me!"

Chapter Notes – Chapter 13

The Plaza de Armas is the main city square of Cusco. It is a beautiful well-manicured park in the northern part of Cusco, and it is the political and religious center of the city. The plaza is fronted by many restaurants, the two main Cathedrals of Cusco, and government and office buildings. The ancient Incan tunnels bisect each other at the Plaza de Armas junction connecting all the important buildings in its path to the fortress of Sacsahuaman on top of the northern hill overlooking Cusco.

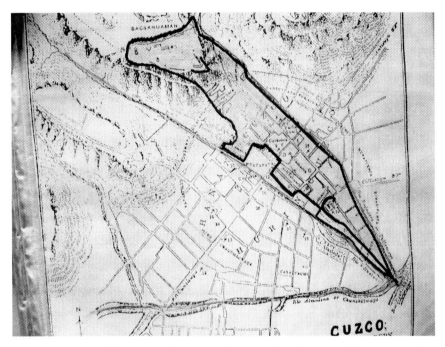

Ancient Map of the City of Cusco showing the design of the city in the form of a Puma, with the Fortress of Sacsahuaman as the top of the head and the Temple of Koricancha as the navel. The temple was the center of the Inca Universe and all roads radiated out from the temple to the rest of the city and to the rest of the empire.

Chapter 14

Inca House Restaurant – Present Day

"Mama, we know about the secret tunnel beneath Cusco because of the Sacred Quipu and where the entrances of the tunnel are. We know which buildings the tunnel goes to and why the Inca sealed it up and why they caved it in. Why can't we tell the world about it? Why does it have to be kept a secret?" Tears were flowing from her big brown eyes. "The Balboa Explorations and Peter now know all about it because of the GPR study. I don't know why we have to keep it secret any longer. Wouldn't it actually be better if we told everyone about it, than to let the foreigners make the discovery in their scientific journals and proclamations to the world?" implored Monica.

"You don't understand, Monica, there is more....I can't tell you.... everything right now. We must protect the secret tunnels at all cost," was her mother's reply.

"But why, Mama...I want to tell Peter everything, why can't I tell Peter at least?" Eva Rodriguez just sadly shook her head. It had been a busy day at the restaurant, and now at lunchtime Monica had much work to do. It would take Monica the full hour to enter everything into the ledger. "I love you Mother. I want to do everything right, but I need to know the reasons." Eva Rodriguez looked at her daughter in total amazement. Oh how she loved this beautiful young woman. "Mama, tell me about my ancestors and especially about Lacoya Ines, the Inca Princess…could you please? Peter says that I look just like her"

"Okay, I'll tell you the story…maybe tonight after work, and we close up the restaurant, we'll have some time," said her mother thoughtfully.

Finally, Eva Rodriguez, turned the key in the lock after she had pulled down the metal- barred security panel that ran the full length of the front of the restaurant's two huge picture windows. She appeared very tired when Monica stood in front of her with that gazing, wanting look of hers. "Are you sure we have to do this tonight?" she asked Monica wearily.

"Yes, mama, I want to know ….I have to know everything," she said with determination. They walked down the hallway arm in arm and up the stairs to their lovely old apartment over top of the restaurant. "Well," she started,"Lacoya Ines, was the legendary very beautiful daughter of the 12th Inca King to reign, Huayna Capac. Actually, he was the last real king of the Inca Empire. The anointed heir to the kingdom was Huascar his oldest son born here in Cusco. Atahualpa was an illegitimate son, born of one of Huayna Capac's concubines who lived in Quito. Atahualpa was mad that he was not chosen to rule, so he fled to his homeland of Quito with many followers. For a few years the empire was divided into the northern kingdom of Quito and the historical kingdom of Cusco. Civil war ravished the Inca nation and nearly destroyed the whole of it." Eva picked up the Sacred Quipu from off its mantel where it was always kept in a special closet. She motioned for her daughter to come and join her on the overstuffed sofa. She caressed a particular knot on one of the lengths of knotted strings, thoughtfully, and continued her story. Monica could picture in her mind the magnificent Inca palace and her beautiful forbearer, Lacoya Ines.

Huayna Capac, the great Inca King had summoned his most favorite daughter, Lacoya Ines, to him. He had recently taken ill with a strange pox, that was previously unknown in the land. "Touch me not, my daughter, I am unclean...you know that I love you most of all my daughters... I have summoned you because I think that I am dying."

"Oh, my father...you can cheat death like you play with the Jaguar... my king!" she burst out lovingly.

"Shhhh now...quickly listen to me. I must ask a favor of you, my daughter."

"Anything,... you know that you can ask me anything..." The heart of the king melted once again and the pounding of a loud drum in his chest was merely the love he had for this gorgeous beloved princess.

"I have received an emissary from Atahualpa," the king continued. "He desires your hand in marriage, my daughter...as a peace offering, a gift...that we might enter into a covenant of peace between us. I am afraid that he will rebel against Huascar and I, and cause this people to go to war against each other if he is not satisfied." He looked up into her sad eyes. He wanted to brush away a tear, but he dared not touch her.

"But, my father," she started to talk softly, "Atahualpa already has four wives, and many concubines, and he does not love me."

"He will," broke in the king. "He will learn to love you as I do because of your goodness and beauty. You must go to him…You must marry him for the sake of the kingdom…It is my loss. I will miss you the most, my love. But, we will meet again in the afterlife."

"I love you, too, my father…I will go and do thy will as you have asked," she said determined to be strong.

"Thank you my love…Thank you."

Four years later, Lacoya Ines was familiar with the Quito palace and her place in Atahualpa's court. His armies had been battling against the forces of the new king, Huascar, for months now. Atahualpa had broken his covenant of peace after the death of his father, the Inca King. Now, his ambition was to rule the whole kingdom not just the northern part of it. They were marching to Cajamarca at the head of his largest army. "Tell me what you have learned?" the Prince demanded of his chief spy.

"The garrison at Cajamarca is small. After our first battle there, we have weakened their army…my King," was the response. "The main force has been called back to regroup with the rest of Huascar's forces. We can take Cajamarca easily, I am sure…my King."

"You have done well…Leave me, now…" barked Atahualpa. "Summon my captains" he again barked to his aide next to him, "We must hold a war council."

Several hours later Atahualpa had his leadership counsel assembled which included his two top generals, Quizquiz and Calicuchima. "We must strike now while we have Huascar's armies in disarray" shouted Atahualpa. He was losing patience with his chief captains and their passive conservative attitude. "Prepare now and meet Huascar's army on the plains of Quepaipa." He commanded them.

"But, Your Greatness,….what of these rumors of the bearded white men that have come among us from the sea?" demanded one of the men.

"Do not worry about them," Atahualpa was shouting loudly again. "I will meet them here at Cajamarca and have them join with us. What threat can they be with only a small handful of men?"

"Maybe their leader is the one that has been prophesied will come to help us conquer?" another general questioned.

"Go now…Prepare and go and meet the enemy, quickly, before we lose our advantage," said Atahualpa angrily. "Quizquiz take the northern army and approach and surround Huascar's army from the north. Calicuchima take the regular Quito army into Quepaipa from the south. The meeting was over abruptly as he stood and glared at his captains defiantly. "Go now…"

"Much happened in the next two months," continued Eva Rodriguez. Atahualpa had been captured by the Spaniards and he was being ransomed and held captive in his own palace in Cajamarca. News of the battle in the plains of Quepaipa was not good. The fighting had been intense on both sides. The armies had decimated each other with neither side holding a distinct advantage. On the last day of battle the army of Atahualpa finished with a slight victory. Many thousands lay dead and their bodies were devoured by wild beasts. The once proud Inca nation was destroyed and scattered to the four winds. It would never rise again to the same might and glory. It had happened all because of the hatred and jealacy of a brother to a brother and a son to his father. Where there should have been love there had been none.

The Spanish had surprised Atahualpa at Cajamarca and captured the Inca monarch. Atahualpa promised to pay a huge ransom in gold and silver treasure in exchange for his freedom. Lacoya Ines was allowed to visit and bring her husband food daily. She was afraid of the Spanish conquistadors, they were brutal mean men who went wild in the city after taking Atahualpa prisoner. Rumors of their raping and pillaging the occupants of the city came from all quarters. So, far the royal family was being spared and protected from the atrocities, however. Nevertheless, she still did not trust them at all. All except one, Hernando, he was called. He was the leader's brother and in charge of their guard. He was a handsome, large young Spaniard somewhat older than what she was; and she knew he liked her. Twice they had met in the hallway leading to Atahualpa's quarters. Each time as she approached, he would kneel on one knee and give her reverence. Each time he had taken her hand in his and kissed it with great emotion. Each time it had sent a tingling sensation up and down her spine. He would look into her eyes and smile with his brilliant white teeth and his neatly trimmed beard. She was quite in love with him. She knew that it wasn't allowed and could never be. But, still…he was so, so handsome.

A week later, Atahualpa had been condemned to death. He sat on the edge of his bed with his only friend, Hernando, "Let me talk to you quietly" Atahualpa began softly in broken Spanish. Lacoya Ines who had been standing near by, was also summoned to the bedside of the Prince as well. "Hernando, my friend, Lacoya Ines is with child …take her as your wife and protect my seed, that my kingdom might live on." She is good and beautiful and she will be a strong woman and a good wife." Lacoya Ines watched as Atahualpa placed her small hand into the large weathered hand of Hernando. His touch again stirred her soul and she seemed to see their hands melt together as her vision blurred through her tears. Atahualpa's Spanish was not good but the message was clear.

"They will not execute you, while I am here. You are a king, a head of state. They would not dare even try you in court without permission from King Charles. I will speak to my brother. He will not allow this to happen!" guaranteed Hernando confidently. Three days later, Hernando was on his way back to San Miguel on the coast with a detail of twenty men conveying the King's treasure back to the coast. Sorrowfully, Atahualpa gave Lacoya Ines to Francisco just before the execution. At noon the next day in the public square of Cajamarca the prince was executed by strangulation, which made Lacoya Ines once again a free single woman.

Two months later, Hernando de Soto was in command of the forward troop approaching Cusco. He and his troop of sixty cavalry were going to enter the city on the next day, and they had set up camp for the night. There were still several hours of daylight, yet. So, he had sent two of his bravest men on ahead into the city to determine the strength of the enemy and the best approach and method to take Cusco. The two spies were dressed in native costume and traveled with a llama so as to not attract attention. They approached Cusco from the south and in the distance as they came over a small rise they noticed a tall tower jutting out from surrounding buildings. The sun was just setting and its rays illuminated the large golden temple next to the tower. The gleaming gold in the sunlight appeared to be glowing like fire. The two conquistadors stood cemented in their tracks, neither could speak. Finally, both in unison declared, "we have found it….El Dorado!"

Francisco Pizarro was with the large main body of the Spanish army that now approached the Inca Capital. They were several days behind de Soto and traveling slowly with the supply train and artillery. The army had halted for the evening to rest and feed the horses and men. Now, Francisco stood hand in hand with Lacoya Ines at a secluded clearing along the same creek that they had camped by further downstream. Francisco turned her into him, "Lacoya Ines do you want to marry me," he asked, "You know that I love you"

"Yes," she quickly said in her broken Spanish. "I promised my father, The Inca, that I would do everything I could to bring peace to my people. He knew that you would come to our land, and set up a new kingdom. So, it is part of my destiny and a dream of my father to bring us together. But, I have made a promise to my people and myself that I would only marry in my own Inca traditions and religion." She said with a concerned look on her face.

"Oh, is that all," Francisco said with a laugh. "Okay…Okay we will do whatever you want when we get into Cusco. You can have an Incan ceremony with your Inca Elders, and I will have a Catholic ceremony with my priest, Valverde, that I have brought with me, and everyone will be happy."

"Really," she said with a smile that totally took his breath away.

"Yes, really...I love you. You are so young and beautiful." Francisco looked into those large brown eyes and kissed her for the first time. Both of them lingered as they tenderly embraced and kissed again. "Tomorrow we will be in Cuzco, and you can prepare for the wedding." Francisco spoke tenderly....

"I am going home...I will be home tomorrow....I can't believe it. I never thought that I would ever see Cusco again," Lacoya Ines cried in delight. "I'm going home tomorrow!"

The conquistadors came over the last rise that looked down over the mountain valley of Cusco. It was the largest city by far that they had seen since landing on the shores of this foreign land. In fact to their astonishment, Cusco appeared to be larger than any of the cities of their homeland country of Spain, even possibly larger than Madrid or Seville. They calculated the number of inhabitants to be well over 300,000 with the surrounding cities to be many more times that number. Their guide motioned to them to follow him. They walked through the crowded Main City Square and down the main street to the South. Most of the people that they saw were women and children. There didn't appear to be an armed Inca warrior in sight. They proceeded down the main cobblestone highway to the south. The conquistadors stood together and at once saw in the distance a large golden building glimmering in the last rays of the setting sun. They stood there spellbound and neither could move. Finally, Hernando de Soto whispered, "We have found it, just like they said, the Golden Temple of El Dorado."

For three days, Hernando de Soto had deployed his 60 troops in securing the city. He had set up his headquarters in the palace of the now dead Inca King, Huascar, without any resistance at all. The rumor among the people was that the princess was coming home and the civil war was over, that peace had finally come to the Highlands of Peru. Not one blunderbuss shot had been fired, no Inca warrior had been seen. What an easy conquest, Cusco, had turned out to be. Francisco Pizarro and Lacoya Ines joined them in Cusco with the rest of the army, except for the garrison that he had left in Catajamarca to maintain that city. They still had their full army intact, and now with the arrival of Almagro's contingent they were 480 strong plus the Canari tribal army. Francisco was anxious for this arrival and the blessing of his upcoming wedding. Surely, this would be a beautiful new home for them. He loved the mountains, he loved the city, but mostly he loved these people he was to govern, especially one lovely Inca Princess.

Diego de Almagro was increasingly angry with the progress of securing the city. "Why have you not done this...Why have you not done that..." was all he could say in his scolding. It upset Francisco immensely, the cold austere attitude that he had toward this people and their city. Almagro had no patience. And worst of all, no compassion for the conquered. "We have been down to the golden temple this morning...we will start dismantling the golden panels off from the walls this afternoon," said Almagro nonchalantly.

"What?"...screamed Francisco, "why?...I told Lacoya Ines that we would not touch or harm her precious Inca temple. She has made peace for us," he said defiantly.

"You're soft...this is what we have come here to do is find gold. We have found it. You need to pull yourself together...you're getting old and weak. I don't want to have to relieve you of your command and send you home to Spain...do I?" Almagro demanded. He looked at his one-time friend with disgust and disdain. "You have really let this native woman affect you…you're too love-sick…get over it, or I will put you in chains, myself," he roared.

Pizarro could feel the heat rising under his own collar and responded angrily. "Diego, you forget yourself. I am the governor, not you."

"No, Francisco I never forget that…Everyday I remember that you are the governor, not me. You may have this woman, do what you want with her….Even marry her with Father Valverde, but she does not rule Peru, we do." With that he whirled around and was gone.

For the first time in weeks, there was a skirmish between the Inca and Spanish. The problem started at the temple as the conquistadors were desecrating the sacred edifice. Many Inca Elders and warriors attacked the Spanish and killed four soldiers before the Spanish could protect themselves and ward off the attack. Francisco and Almagro acted quickly and rounded up as many Inca as they could find that were involved in the attack and executed them in the main city square. Almagro even executed some people without Pizarro's knowledge that had nothing to do with the skirmish as a warning against further problems and as a show of force to the Inca. From then on, Francisco Pizarro placed guards around the Temple of Koricancha to protect the workers and also to safeguard the temple treasure.

"We must do this quietly, " Francisco whispered, "did you talk to the Inca Elder to come and perform the wedding? I will not take you unto me tonight until we are wed. I love you so much. But, it wouldn't be fair to you, and I have made a promise to you forever," he said sweetly.

"We must hurry, ...everything is in readiness. We are to meet the Elder in the Sun Room of the Temple of Koricancha where he will perform the marriage. Here at the entrance of the temple courtyard we must take off our shoes. Because where we stand and go from here is 'Holy Ground'. Remember that the temple is a sacred place," whispered back the princess. Lacoya Ines was dressed in a breath-taking white vicuna wedding dress made just for this occasion. The Elder dressed in his ceremonial temple garments, tied their right hands together with a woolen string laced with golden threads and uttered several brief incantations in the Quechua language. At the end of the ceremony, Francisco took Lacoya Ines firmly in his arms and kissed her passionately. Oh, how he loved her.

"Good thing the temple guard found some Chicha that was left abandoned this evening," chuckled Francisco. "Quickly, let us return to the palace before anyone misses us..."

"Wait," whispered Lacoya Ines, she took the wedding band off from her hand and tied it to the Quipu around the Elder's neck and tied a knot in the string for the rememberer.

Lacoya Ines was only now starting to show that she was with child. Now, that she and Francisco were living as husband and wife, then Almagro would never know that she was carrying Atahualpa's child. Just as in Cajamarca, Pizarro allowed his men to rape and pillage where they may, even with Lacoya Ines's protests over such behavior. The first order of business was to secure as much treasure as they could find. It took several weeks to dismantle the more than 700 golden panels from the Temple of Koricancha and to gather all of the gold and silver that could be found in the city. The eventual total treasure was many times more than the ransom acquired at Cajamarca. A temporary smelter was set up to melt all of the incredible Inca artifacts down into gold bullion. A fifth of the tally would be again carried back to the new supply city, San Miguel. The generals got a generous portion in the dispersal, the Calvary or horsemen received double the booty of the infantry in the accounting. Never, had a group of ordinary soldiers ever get so rich so quickly. For most their riches were very temporary, and were relieved of their person by a simple throw of a dice or some other game of chance. The treasure shipment went to the port at Tumbes from San Miguel for shipment to Panama City and finally back to Spain. Two fifths was saved out for Francisco Pizarro and the colonial government maintenance, and the other two fifths were distributed equally among all of the 480 Spanish conquistadors present in Cusco according to their various station in life. Never had a few adventurers ever become so wealthy overnight. Pizarro because of his age was affected greatly from the altitude sickness and he and his wife decided to move to the coast for his health. Francisco left Hernando Pizarro and his other brothers in charge of the city of Cusco. He moved his headquarters to the newly built capital city, Lima, and established his government and built a sumptuous palace there.

"But mama whatever happened to Lacoya Ines," said Monica in a sleepy voice, laying her head on her mother's lap.

"She had three children and lived with the governor, Francisco, for several years in Lima. "They were very happy together, and rejoiced in their children," continued her mother. The Spanish and Inca ruled this city and Peru together in peace for many years. Eventually, other royal Inca descendants rebelled against the Spanish rule and there were many wars. Francisco, governed from Lima with an iron hand and was a hard and brutal taskmaster, he was eventually assassinated by his own men in his Lima palace while he sat at dinner with his friends." Eva mused as she caressed the knot of a beautiful golden string. Monica was asleep in her lap. "Would she ever be able to tell her everything?" Eva smiled speaking to herself, "Someday....maybe someday."

Chapter Notes – Chapter 14

The Spanish Conquistadors entered the Inca Capital on November 15, 1533 exactly one year to the day of the massacre at Cajamarca. The conquest of Peru was essentially complete. It was far easier to destroy temples and palaces, and unfortunately the Spanish spent the next three centuries trying to destroy the Incan Culture, but could not. Possession of the City of Cusco occurred without a gunshot fired. Francisco Pizarro married the Inca Princess, Lacoya Ines. Their first child, a daughter, was named Francisca after her father, the first governor of Peru.

A scale model of Santa Domingo, the modern Catholic Cathedral and Monestary that now sits on top of the most sacred spot of the Inca Culture, the Temple of Koricancha.

Chapter 15

Cusco – Present Day

Peter had stuck to his plan. He had avoided Monica for a whole week, now. Peter was beginning to think that he was right; that a little distance from her and he would be able to think clearly and react responsibly when he had to work with her again. It was a splendid plan, she did phone and leave a couple of messages at his apartment, but he didn't have to actually speak with Monica. Peter knew that he had a definite weakness for the Peruvian black-haired beauty. So, if he could just avoid her as much as possible then he would be better off. And maybe, he would be able to survive this Peruvian Project after all and return home to California and rebuild his life.

Meanwhile, Peter had begun with his study of the Temple of Koricancha, itself. He studied the foundation stones. Peter studied the three rooms that were still left intact, the temples of the sun, moon, and stars. The more he got into it the more it intrigued him. This was a special building that dated from at least 580 B.C. The stonework was exquisite and polished to a higher degree than any other building in Pre-Inca history. The temple was originally given to Hernando Pizarro in the first distribution of properties to the conquistadores in 1538. Then, Hernando had donated the building to the Dominican Order of the Catholic Church at the insistence of his brother, Francisco. Hernando wanted to honor a commitment that he had made with Lacoya Ines that he would keep sacred the temple. So, he compromised with the priests. They promised to not destroy the temple, but to build their cathedral over the top of the temple walls and leave the temple intact. Therefore, the Dominicans built a chapel and monastery over top of the temple using the walls and other smaller rocks for foundation of the new colonial church. The Santa Domingo Church during the next four hundred years had to be rebuilt twice because of earthquakes. The last time was in 1950 when the monastery was completely destroyed and this time pains were taken to not build directly on top of the remaining Inca walls, but the Catholic church structure still encompassed the Inca Temple with only the round Sun Room exposed to the outside and to public view. It soon became a work of love and Peter was enthralled with these ancient artisans that could have built such a structure without mortar, or modern tools using this very hard Andesite stone.

Peter was spending so much time in the Koricancha Temple from the public opening to closing time at night, that he made friends with two of the Dominican Priests. Peter gleaned a lot of knowledge about the structure itself and the history of Koricancha from the priests. It had become evident that these ancient structures and stone work were not the recent work of the Inca empire, but of ancient origin with the Chavin Culture. Peter read and studied as much material as he could get his hands on. The priests were good men and they taught him a lot, too. Peter understood their claim and their insistence to maintain their exclusive rights to the property. After all, it appeared that the temple wasn't in fact built by the Inca people as he had once thought. The Church had received UNESCO international historical monument status on all their cathedrals and churches in Cusco because they are over 400 years old. They are now protected by UNESCO, and the Santa Domingo Monastery is no exception, even if it was built over the top of the most Sacred Incan Temple in all of South America. It was the naval or center of their universe…The Golden Temple of the Sun. If Cusco was built in the form of a Puma, then Koricancha was situated to be at the place of the Puma's navel. The center of the Inca Capital City, and originally the center of the Capital of the Chavin Empire as well.

One of the priests related a story of a young man who found the entrance to the secret tunnel under Koricancha and after several days he found his way back to the entrance completely delirious and sick clutching a magnificent golden cob of corn in his hand. The young man died and the priests melted the artifact down and made it into a crown for the Bishop of Cusco to silence the rumors of the secret tunnels. The priest showed Peter the Crown in its display case in the monastery.

Peter was one day working in the Sun Room. He was checking out the sun stones that were used to tell the seasons and time of day. "This is just incredible," Peter kept telling himself. He heard footsteps on the stone floor in front of him. Monica was standing there smiling with the full dimples in her cheeks that he just loved.

"Hi," she said, "I've missed you."

"I know…I know…I've been working pretty hard." It was all that Peter could say to her.

"Why aren't you wearing any shoes?" Monica blurted out.

"Didn't you know that where you stand is sacred ground? You are not supposed to wear shoes anywhere within two hundred feet of the temple grounds. This place is incredible. I've learned so much. There is a special feeling that I have when I'm in here. I don't know what it is. I can't quite put my finger on it. But I'm spending way too much time, here because I just can't get over the feeling that I have working in the temple.

"You want to take a break for a few minutes? I brought some sandwiches…" Monica said with a grin.

"Sure," he couldn't believe how apprehensive he was about having her here. They wandered back out to the Temple Garden and to their park bench, walking the few hundred paces in silence. Peter bought two soft drinks from a nearby vendor and they began their lunch. For twenty minutes they sat and ate in relative silence.

"Peter, I'm sorry if I said something wrong…I didn't mean to hurt you or offend you….What's the matter?" Monica began.

"I don't want to talk about it, really…," sighed Peter.

"Come on, Peter, remember this is your friend, Monica, tell me what's wrong?" she said as she placed her hand on top of his. He did not have the strength to take his hand away, he was too weak…he knew it. "Tell me…I know I can help."

"Hmmm…I don't know…If you really want to know about my problems." Peter sighed.

"Sure I do. I just want to help," encouraged Monica.

"My girlfriend, Shelley, is engaged! ...**ENGAGED!**...Can you believe, that. I was kidnapped and out of touch for a month, and that's what I get, for it," blurted out Peter. He had said it almost before he knew it. Peter had vented and then immediately he was sorry he had confided all of this problem with Shelley to Monica.

Monica gasped and instinctively put one hand over her mouth. Monica picked up his hand and squeezed it, tightly. "Oh, I'm sorry, Peter, I truly am...I didn't know...I'm sorry," she said sincerely. "How can I cheer you up?" Monica thought pensively for a moment, then said, "I know just the thing...It's a secret. You can't tell my mother that I have shown it to you. Come with me, Peter! I have something to show you," she said enthusiastically.

"But...But...I can't ....I'm working here...can't you see that," he said doggedly.

"Oh, Peter..." She leaned over and gave him a quick peck on the cheek. "I'm sure that the Temple will be here tomorrow and you can finish then. It's already more than twenty-five hundred years old, now. This won't wait. We have to go now while my mother is busy in the restaurant." Monica was pretty determined and he simply couldn't resist her, anyway.

"Okay, let's go," Peter smiled back at her for the first time, and it encouraged her.

"Great!"

Monica was practically running up the street the three blocks to the main city square, Plaza de Armas, with Peter in tow. "Hey, what can be so important, where are we going?" Peter kept questioning completely out of breath. He didn't mind holding her hand, but she was being so mysterious, and captivating at the same time, and this was exactly the type of situation that he was trying to avoid with her. She just kept sucking him in to her closer all the time and his weakness for her did not let him resist her strength over him. He was definitely into some major quicksand, here. They both reached the restaurant completely out of breath with their lungs burning because of the altitude. Instead of going in the front door, Monica directed him to a side entrance, that Peter did not know existed. They crept inside and down a set of stairs to what appeared to be a basement storage room.

Monica moved quickly to the back of the room. She said, "hurry, Peter, we need to unload the boxes and cans in this storage cabinet." When the cabinet was empty, Peter helped Monica slide it out from against the wall.

"It's a secret door!" Peter exclaimed. "Where does it lead to?" They opened the old wooden door together. A small dark opening emerged from behind the door. "Wow!" Peter was really excited, now.

"It's an entrance to the secret tunnels of Cusco," Monica said proudly.

"Wow! This is incredible… and here I thought that you were leading me…," Peter started to laugh.

"Mister Martin!" Monica cut in. "Leading you, where?" she laughed, too. He grabbed her with the intention of giving her a big Peruvian hug. But he missed...or stumbled off balance, and instead their faces came together and instantly his lips had found hers....the miracle was that she acted as if she enjoyed it. But, she started giggling in the middle and Peter pulled back. He looked into those big brown eyes, truly confused.

"Oh, Peter, that is the worst kiss that I have ever had. And I was really looking forward to it, for weeks..." she giggled again.

"What are you talking about...that was wonderful! It was a Peruvian hug and Californian kiss all in one move! I'll bet no one has ever done that to you before, right?" Peter observed bravely.

"You're right, nobody has ever done it like that before!..."

"Okay...Okay..."cut in Peter. He slid his arm around her slender waist and drew her closer, looking right down into her beautiful eyes. "Well... maybe I should try again!" he teased. Peter awkwardly turned away from her to close the wooden door.

Now, it was Peter's turn to hold Monica's hand tightly as he started to lead her upstairs and into the restaurant. Peter stopped. "Monica, why didn't you tell me that you knew where this tunnel entrance was before? You've known about this all along, haven't you?" queried Peter sternly.

"Oh, Peter, I wanted to tell you all along, but I have promised my Mother. It is part of the teachings of the Sacred Quipu that I told you about, before. I am committed to keep it secret. It is a sacred part of our history and our culture. You must promise to keep it secret, too! It is important or they will not let me be the next 'rememberer', after my mother."

"Why should I keep it secret? You deceived me. You knew about it, and you didn't tell me. You didn't trust me," Peter said seriously.

"I showed it to you because you were sad and lonely. I just wanted to please you," Monica said with a coy little grin. "And, because you love me, you'll keep it a secret won't you?" she giggled again at his expression.

"I'm still hungry," he joked back at her. "And, we are at a restaurant." Then Peter turned her around and with a serious look held her by the hand. "Monica, we need to go in and explore it," he said excitedly.

"No, Peter, we can't…no one who has ever gone into the tunnels have ever come back alive. That is why the conquistadors, the Inca, and the priests all sealed up the entrances centuries ago. There are poisonous gases in there. I won't let you," Monica implored.

"Monica, we have to go in and explore it." He was not discouraged by her comments at all.

"**NO!**"… Her voice was angry now.

"Okay, I'll find a way for us to be safe and protected, before we go in. Peter looked back at the storage room. Help me put the cabinet back together." Peter pleaded. They returned back to the cabinet and started to restock the shelves the way they were before. "You've known about it all along?" Peter asked questioningly.

"Yes, it's part of the secrets of the Sacred Quipu, that I keep telling you about. My mother is the keeper of the Sacred Quipu, the 'rememberer'. I will be the 'rememberer' some day if I am worthy, and we are supposed to guard the secrets with our lives. I shouldn't tell you anymore. I just wanted to make you happy and lift your spirits. You are my friend, you know. You will keep this secret, won't you?" Monica begged him.

"Sure, but ...eventually, the Balboa Explorer will tell the world about the secrets of the tunnels of Cusco. So, it won't matter...What else do you know? How many other entrances are still open to the tunnels? What is down there?" Peter was going a hundred miles an hour.

"Whoa...hold your horses...I don't think I'll tell you anymore...My mom is going to kill me if she finds out I showed you the entrance....I don't know if I can trust you anymore..."she said sadly.

"I'm sorry...Okay, so I got a little carried away. Let's eat...I'm starved," grinned Peter.

Peter was so excited about the tunnel entrance that the next morning he left his boarding house early and took a cab to the military post and asked to see General Rojas. He hadn't checked in with the police or the military yet today so he thought that he would just go in person to see the general.

The army general, General Rojas, looked at him inquisitively, "Sure, we have protective suits and portable breathing apparatus."

"Could we borrow two sets?" pressed Peter.

"Well, now, I should probably know why, and what you're up to. You seem to get into lots of trouble here in Cusco and I don't want to be responsible for any more problems that you will get into," said the general thoughtfully.

"Okay, it's for a good cause…., grinned Peter."

"What…, that's it, …it's for a good cause? Next time, I will buy breakfast, then I can require you to give me more information…Come by the Supply Depot this afternoon and I will have someone check you out with the equipment," said the general reluctantly.

"Thanks General Rojas, you won't be sorry, and we'll be careful with your equipment … Thanks," said Peter gratefully.

Chapter Notes – Chapter 15

The Koricancha Temple or Temple of the Sun was built by the Chavin Culture approximately 580B.C. The temple is the holiest, most sacred ancient temple in all of South America. The Inca people revere it even to the modern day as their most sacred site. When Pizarro entered Cusco, the temple was clad with 700 sheets of gold usually measuring about two foot by four foot in dimension and about a quarter of an inch thick. The temple was adorned with a huge amount of silver and gold artifacts, jewels and precious stones. There was also a large golden disc in the center of the Sun Room wall that became a prized treasure of a lucky conquistador. There are four out of the seven original rooms still standing. The temple walls are built of finely polished Andesite stone in an 'Egyptian Style' where the base stones are thicker at the bottom and gradually grow smaller on each rising concourse. The walls appear to be leaning, but such construction has made the temple virtually earthquake proof. Many scholars have said that the Temple of Koricancha was built after the manner of the Temple of Solomon.

The ancient tunnels of the City of Cusco were built early on in the history of the city. These legendary tunnels were sealed up by the Spanish conquistadors in the early sixteenth century for safety sake. Everyone that entered the tunnels perished because of the deadly atmosphere that existed in the tunnels. So, all entrances were sealed or the tunnel caved in to prevent any other adventurers losing their lives.

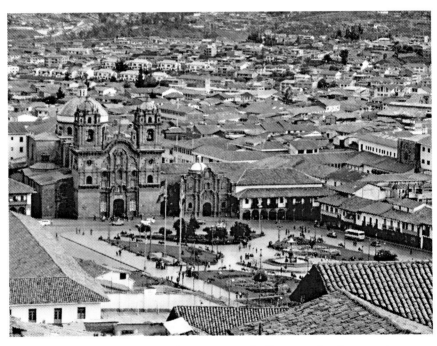

A view of the Plaza de Armas with Cusco in background

Chapter 16

Cusco Restaurant – Present Day

Monica was waiting for Peter at the side entrance of the restaurant at 2:00pm in the afternoon, when he pulled up in the cab. She helped him unload the equipment and take it inside. They went downstairs and slid the cabinet away from the wall to expose the secret door. "Monica," Peter started, "we need to have a good plan, here so that we can do everything safely. I've got protective suits and gloves for us, two good flashlights, and two complete portable breathing air units."

"I'm not sure that we should do this," Monica said slowly and reluctantly. "Maybe we should forget the whole thing."

Peter whistled softly, "Monica, this is going to be fantastic, an adventure of a lifetime. I promise we'll be safe...you just stay close to me at all times, and you'll be fine." He squeezed her hand softly. "Come on it will be fun." He started to unpack everything on the basement floor.

"Maybe you should go and I'll stay here at the doorway and wait for you to get back," she said cautiously.

"Monica," Peter said sternly, "you can't back out, now. We agreed to do this together, actually… remember that this is all your idea."

"Okay, let's go and do it," she said softly in a tiny voice.

"I have my digital camera and a compass, and my GPR map of the city. We are here on the map." Peter pointed to a dot on the map. The Cusco Cathedral which was once the Inca palace is here only 200 yards away to the west at the intersection of the lines. Here is where the tunnel turns south to the Temple of Koricancha. Our goal is to see if we can make it to the palace. It is now almost three o'clock p.m. I will mark the time when we go in. We will only have thirty minutes after we enter the tunnel, only fifteen minutes in then we will need to start back no matter what, Okay? Any questions?" Peter grinned. He was so excited, the adrenaline had already kicked in, and he was speaking faster and faster.

"Slow down," Monica said with a frown.

"Do you have any questions?" Peter asked.

"Yea, one…will you promise me that you will bring me back home safe and sound?" she said earnestly.

"I will bring you home safe, I promise…"Peter looked into her face for a long moment, and then he lifted his hand and lovingly touched her cheek. A mischievous smile appeared, and he quickly said, "maybe you will have to be the one to drag me back to the entrance!" Peter laughed. That little indiscretion was reciprocated immediately with a blow to his shoulder. "Ouch…" he winced with mock pain.

Peter cautioned and repeated the instructions again, "we only have thirty minutes of air in these tanks when you breathe normally. So, I have this timer here that will ring when we have used half of our air.

"Okay, okay….you've already told me all this!" Monica was annoyed with how much fun Peter was having with all of this. "Are you sure you want to go through with this?"

Peter just gave Monica a tired disdainful look. "Monica you promised me…" with that little look Peter just picked up the instruction where he left off like he had never been interrupted. "We will need to start back when we come to the halfway point. We have a five minute emergency supply in this small bottle. Let me fit this mask to your face." Peter spent the next ten minutes explaining the operation of the equipment and putting it on her and letting her breathe for a few moments in a trial run. He was surprised how quick a learner Monica was. She was quickly warming up to the whole experience and getting excited about the adventure. Peter helped her get into the protective suit. It was an interesting experience trying to stuff all of her beautiful long dark hair into the suit and brushing it back from her face to fit the mask on her again. He checked the mask fit again with a negative pressure test, to make sure that no poisonous gases could harm her. He placed the hood over her, and then quickly put all of his suit and equipment on as well. This was getting good….

"Monica it is now 3:17. We need to be back by 3:47!" Peter yelled through the mask. Peter swung the door open and they were inside. Inside their suits they could not feel the cool damp air of the tunnel. It was still a weird sensation to step inside the tunnel. Peter flicked on his light. The passage way was narrow only about three feet wide with a low ceiling and in places Peter had to lower his head. Peter turned around to make sure Monica was alright. He smiled at her and said to her with a muffled voice, "let's go."

The tunnel almost immediately made a sharp turn to the right and about twenty steps down into a long narrow passage way. The passage way opened into the main tunnel which widened and led straight for a long distance. According to Peter's compass reading they were heading west and in the direction that they wanted to go. It was easy going, in this wider tunnel. Peter was encouraged and they were making good progress. Another fifty feet and they came to a wider opening, a small room, really. Peter shone his light around the room inspecting it closely. It was completely empty. Peter was quickly to the other side of the room and through the entrance and then deeper down the tunnel. Monica, was slower, she was finding the bulkiness of the suit and the heavy breathing equipment to be quite annoying. She was at least ten feet behind Peter as she emerged from the room her foot brushed something in the dark. At once a cloud of dust enveloped her as she slipped to the tunnel floor. Monica shrieked… Heavy objects fell on her and around her, with muffled sounds. She shone her light around her as she sat up. Terrified with what she saw she screamed again. There were two dead bodies laying on her, skeletons really. The leathern faces of the skulls had hideous, wretched expressions of terror. Her own heart was pounding furiously and her terror matched those of the dead. Peter was immediately there at her side. "Hummm…looks like these guys have been here a while, doesn't look like they made it out in time!" Peter commented jokingly in muffled tones, as he cleared away the skeletons for Monica so that she could stand up.

"I don't think that is funny at all," Monica said in disgust. "These poor men…" she said sorrowfully. They continued down the hallway.

"Monica, you have to control your breathing…you can't get so excited. You have to breathe normally otherwise your air won't last as long." Peter warned with a loud voice.

"Sure that's easy for you to say," she countered loudly.

The tunnel was pretty straight. They had gone at least 100 to 150 feet already. It couldn't be more than 50 to another 100 feet to the palace area. Peter could see that the path went down hill a little and twenty feet a head was another opening in the tunnel. This black wide expanse was quite a bit larger than the first room. Peter threw the light from his flashlight around the room. This room was not empty, but contained rusted and cankered shields, swords, and ancient weapons of war of all kinds, shapes, and sizes. There were also more skeletons of men dressed in armor, and some that wore long textile robes. Two animal corpses were in one corner that looked like llamas or vicunas. When Monica entered the room with her light, she immediately gasped, "Look at all of this" she exclaimed. Peter took out his camera and took several pictures.

Again the passage seemed to go down in elevation. Peter took Monica by the hand; there was nothing but cold plastic in the grasp. The sensation felt funny to him and he felt cheated somehow. The passage way was straight again and they made their way for another thirty feet. Then there was nothing only blackness of a stone wall stared back at Peter in the light. An alarm sounded inside his suit, it made Peter jump. For the first time on their little escapade, it gave Peter a moment of fright. He feverishly hunted for the button on the alarm to shut it off. "Wow, had it really been fifteen minutes, already?" he thought incredulously. Finally, Peter successfully turned off the irritating noise, and he turned to Monica and motioned the other way. "Time to head back," came his muffled voice. Monica, just stood there looking past him.

"Just a little further, please Peter," she implored loudly. Peter just looked at her with a questioning stare and lowering eyebrows and a shrug of his shoulders he moved ahead. Right at the stone wall face there was an immediate turn to the right. Another large room loomed before them, it was an incredible huge area. Peter paused for a moment to shine his light around him. As far as he could see were golden statues, vases, and various other golden artifacts all shinning back to them in the glimmering light. As far as they could see in the limited light of their flashlights were objects of all shapes and sizes lined along the sides of this huge long room. With mouths wide open in awe, they continued to proceed through the room to the far end. Peter was taking pictures furiously with his digital camera as they moved through the room. They could not speak….it was totally incredible…truly amazing.

Peter stopped abruptly and Monica came up to stand by his side, she also stopped short. Before them, were two elegantly crafted golden thrones with precious stones inlaid into the golden metallurgy, standing against the far wall. On the royal chairs sat the remains of two mummified personages, one obviously a Spanish conquistador with all his armor still intact and the other a long-haired woman. Peter moved closer and shone his light more fully upon them. They both gasped at once when they saw their fingers intertwined as they held each other's hands. Peter took his camera out of his satual again and began snapping pictures in earnest. Monica just stood there with her flashlight… mesmerized …she was in shock…."This was my ancestor, the Princess Lacoya Ines," she forced out through a muffled squeal of delight.

Peter stowed his camera, grabbed up his flashlight, and grabbed Monica's hand, all in one motion. "We've got to go," he yelled at her through his plastic hood, and breathing mask. They turned around and retraced their steps moving quickly.

At the turn in the passage way where the light from the restaurant basement illuminated the tunnel floor, another alarm was sounding. It was the five minute warning signal saying that the air in Peter's cylinder was gone and that he just had reserve air left. They were through the door and Peter quickly took off the hood and then removed his air mask. He then helped Monica off with her equipment and suit. She was laughing, "That was wonderful, …no, it was simply incredible. I can't believe it. We need to go back." Monica was so excited she was jumping up and down with little hopping motions.

"Slow down," Peter soothed as he put his hands up to take hold of her boots. He noticed that her hair was all matted and wet. "You're a real sight," he giggled. Peter put his arms about her. She smelled of sweat mingled with rose perfume of some kind.

At once he was conscience of his own personal hygiene. "You're not anything to write home about, either," she laughed quickly. "Oh, Peter, wasn't it wonderful…." She had her arms around him and squeezed him tightly.

"No," he was looking into the caverns of her large dark eyes, …you're wonderful…" he said lovingly. "I would have come back without finding anything at all! You were the one who wanted to go on a little further after the alarm sounded. You're incredible."

Peter had all the equipment lugged up the stairs, and he had just stepped outside to hail a cab. Monica opened the door to the restaurant with all the equipment at her feet, to see if the coast was clear and to see if anyone had been watching. There in front of her stood her mother. "**Monica!!!**, ….what have you done?"

Chapter Notes – Chapter 16

According to the Ground Penetrating Radar (GPR) study done in 2000, the tunnel extends for some three kilometers roughly along the Avenue of the Sun (Avenida del Sol). The line goes from the southern end of the old city to the northern end terminating at the fortress of Sacsahuaman on top of the hill. The tunnel also radiates east and west connecting all the important Incan palaces and buildings bisecting at the Plaza de Armas.

Panoramic view of the Fortress of Sacsahuaman which protected the city of Cusco

Chapter 17

Upstairs in Monica's home – Modern Day

"Monica, you have violated your oath and commitment to the Sacred Quipu. I cannot trust you anymore. You have disappointed me, and betrayed your Inca roots. I don't want you to have anything to do with this American, Peter, anymore." They were seated in their upstairs living room, positioned across from each other.

Monica had been crying and her eyes were red and her face flushed. "Mother it's all my fault. It was my idea," cried Monica. "I showed Peter the tunnel. I owe him a lot. I owe him my life. He was depressed and upset about losing his girlfriend back home, and I was trying to cheer him up and make him happy. I'm sorry… I did the wrong thing. I should have listened to you. But, Mother….I think I love him! No, I know I love him." A sudden realization gripped her heart. "Oh, mama, what should I do?" Again, she was sobbing.

"Monica, you know that you can't marry him. It is impossible. You have an obligation to your family, to your people," said her mother with compassion. "Monica, you and Peter have disturbed a sacred place where our ancestors have rested in peace for many centuries. It is one of the most sacred of all of our Inca religious and historical traditions to reverence the dead and their final resting places. The 'rememberers' have recorded these things in the Sacred Quipu. Now, I am worried that you are not worthy to become a 'rememberer'. I cannot allow you to marry someone not of Peruvian descent, especially not some American stranger. You are of royal Inca birth, you have an obligation to your people, to carry on the royal line of ancestry. Only your Uncle Carlos's family carries the same pure blood line. You are the eldest in your generation, and the right to rule should go to you. I am concerned that once I tell him of what has happened then he will ask the elders to take away your privilege and give it to his own children," said Eva Rodriguez soberly.

"Uncle Carlos knows about the Sacred Quipu?" questioned Monica.

"Yes, my daughter, he knows everything. He is my younger baby brother and my father and mother placed all these responsibilities upon me because he was too young. He has never been instructed in the Sacred Quipu. But, now it will fall to him," Eva lamented.

"What if Peter loves me? What if Peter decides he wants to marry me? I can't turn my back on him. I love him. What is wrong with marrying him? The ancestral line will still live on in our children," cried Monica fervently.

"Shhhh…." broke in Monica's mother. "I won't allow it. He is not worthy. He cannot be trusted to keep sacred our traditions and our history. Peter came here to excavate, exploit, and violate our temple and our secret tunnels. Your uncle is in position to maintain and protect their sacred nature from the world," explained Eva Rodriguez.

"What are you saying, Mother?" Monica asked incredulously. "Uncle Carlos is the Director of Tourism. He is supposed to be helping me get permits to excavate the tunnels and expose them to the world for the sake our tourism industry."

"Monica, your Uncle Carlos placed you in your position, and he is in his tourism position to ensure the exact opposite. Over the years the elders and I have worked diligently to make sure that we have the right people in place to make sure that all these Sacred Inca traditions and artifacts are kept safe from the world. Someday the power of the Church will decline or will be extinguished, the corrupt government will be replaced by responsible people, and we will receive the Temple of the Sun back to the Inca people," explained Monica's mother fervently.

" Mother, I have worked so hard these past months for all these things and now you are telling me that they are not what the Inca people want. I can't believe it. I feel like I have wasted these past months. Why didn't you tell me these things before? Why?" asked Monica passionately.

"Your uncle assured us that it would be impossible to get the permits anyway from the priests, so it wouldn't matter what you did. It was impossible. The Department of Tourism and the city needed the publicity and the notoriety to ensure they received the money from the Peruvian government financing for these projects. These funds would go directly into the city coffers, for the benefit of the city and the people," Eva responded kindly to her daughter.

"I can't believe this," whispered Monica wearily. "I'm tired. I'm going to bed." Monica realized suddenly that she was very tired, and it had all given her a headache.

In the beautiful temple garden, Monica tried to explain to Peter the situation. The early morning sun had not warmed the earth, yet. There were still cloudy mists that floated up from the flower beds and wet grass areas. It was going to be a clear, hot sunny day. Peter was really unsure why he was here so early in the morning. "Monica, I don't understand this at all. I thought your mother liked me the other day. We hit it off fabulously in the restaurant. What have I done wrong? Sure, we went into the tunnel, but eventually the whole world will know about it," Peter sighed.

"Peter, I am her only daughter, her only child left in this life. I am her only family. I think she is scared, and over protective of me. I think she is worried about you, and what your intentions are," she said as she looked at him intently. "What are your intentions, anyway?"

"What do you mean?" asked Peter with an astonished look on his face. "Haven't I been a gentleman? I haven't done…"

"No, that's not what I mean," broke in Monica. "Besides, what are your intentions? How do you feel about me?" Monica said with a coy smile. There it was. It was now out in the open. It was the discussion that Peter was trying to avoid. Peter was hoping that he could somehow finish his project, and jump on that plane bound for California without opening this can of worms. He was hoping he could leave all these confrontations in his own mind and the feelings of his heart in Peru and not have to deal with them or take them back with him to California.

Somehow he knew he was going to get hurt and that it would be too painful. Besides hadn't he suffered enough lately with love sickness. Did he really need to do this again, at least so soon? Life was proving to be pretty brutal and detrimental to his fragile psyche. "I guess I like you," was his delayed wounded response.

"Like me? Are you sure that's all?" She came back with a puffed-out lower lip and puppy-dog face.

"Okay... I like you a lot. Is that a crime?" Peter said defiantly. "I don't know why you're hounding me. I don't know why you had us kidnapped on my first day in town and then made me rescue you, twice. You've been unfair to me, and have the advantage. I'm just here to work and do a job. Besides, you're Mother hates me, now." reviewed Peter.

"Oh, Peter," she said as she jumped up and flew into his arms and kissed him tenderly.

Peter went back to work all morning trying to finish up his Koricancha Temple survey so that he could move on to other sites. Monica had returned from her office to visit with him. "I need to take a break. Let's go into the museum office. I want to show you the pictures that I took inside the tunnel." Peter said enthusiastically. For the next hour, they both had a fun time studying the pictures carefully, and reliving the incredible experience of their tunnel adventure. "You know we need to go back and do it again," Peter said. He was gazing at this beautiful Peruvian girl with her nice blue business suit. Peter had never seen this suit before, but it was already his favorite, because it accentuated her generous figure and was just his favorite color. "Man you're beautiful. Did I tell you how much I like your outfit today?" Peter soothed.

"Yes, you told me that twice already this morning." Monica smiled at him. She knew Peter kept saying it because it made her blush and he just wanted to see her response and make her embarrassed. "I'm just wondering if you love my outfit or if you love me!" She laughed as she watched Peter's jaw drop open in astonishment. "Come on, let's get back to work." Monica coaxed. He would focus on the task at hand, again. He was almost done with his research and study of the Temple of Koricancha and he was now doing some mapping and work on the garden itself. His plan was to next do a complete study of the fortress of Sacsahuaman. Tomorrow, Peter would start on the fortress and the possible openings or entrances that existed, there.

It was a gloomy cloudy morning. Monica and Peter had started early and worn rain coats because of the rainy weather forecast. The Fortress had three ancient towers or foundations to the towers that would have served as the command posts at the top of the hillside fortress. Sacsahuaman was really one of the most impressive of all the Inca ruins not just because of its beauty and stone construction, but because of its size and magnitude. There were three tiers of colossal stones fit together so precisely that a knife blade cannot be inserted between them, and laid together without mortar. This was incredible to Peter. Each tier was about 1800 feet long and 18 feet high built in a zig zag pattern for defensive purposes. It was truly a fine fortress, built to protect the city of Cuzco and was used as a refuge in times of war for the Cuscanos.

Monica was acting as Peter's assistant. She had the job of writing down measurements on his clipboard. They had many hours of fun just walking around the colossal structure holding hands and talking endlessly. With the added help, Peter had largely completed the fortress project in less than three days. Peter had identified three possible places where the Balboa Explorations could begin excavations to find entrances to the tunnels in the fortress. "Let's go for supper. Do you think that your Mom will mind if she sees you with me at the restaurant?" questioned Peter.

"Oh, I don't think that is such a good idea, Peter. Maybe we should go to a different restaurant. I know another really nice little place that is also owned by our family," said Monica with her beautiful dimpled smile.

"Sounds great.... I'm famished," exclaimed Peter. They picked out a nice secluded table with the waitress, who was a friend of Monica. "Could you please bring me a huge milanesa steak as soon as possible?" blurted out Peter before he even sat down. The short stocky young woman looked at him and just laughed.

"So, this is why I never see you and why you don't come to the restaurant any more," she giggled as she looked at Monica. Monica just stood there astonished.

"Sorry," Peter apologized as he stood back up to take Monica's chair and help her get seated. Now, he was really embarrassed after having forgotten his manners altogether because of famine. "Why can't we go back down into the tunnel," continued Peter after the waitress had taken their orders and left again.

"I told you, she doesn't trust me, anymore. Mother has locked the basement storeroom door and only she has the key," she said in an agitated tone.

"This is totally unfair. We are sitting on one of the most fabulous discoveries in modern history and we can't do anything about it," frowned Peter. "It's the Martin family legacy, actually. For two centuries my family sat on the property of the great Californian gold rush, and we never did anything with it." Now, it was Peter's turn to be upset and frustrated. "At some point, the Spanish consortium will get a permit to enter the tunnels from someone and the secret will be out and it will be broadcast to the world. I promise, you. It will happen," said Peter fervently.

Monica looked at him compassionately, she knew that she was in love with him. "I know…. I know. However, I am sworn to protect the temple and the tunnels for my people. I better not help you anymore. It's too confusing for me. My mother doesn't want me to have anymore to do with you and maybe she is right. I am basically a peacemaker by nature, and I really just want to make everyone happy. I owe you a lot, Peter. We have become good friends and I care for you," Monica sobbed in a small voice. Peter couldn't believe his ears. He knew it. He now cared for this Peruvian beauty deeply and he had opened up his heart again just to have it trampled on. He felt like some Inca Elder had him laying on the sacrificial altar and had just ripped out his heart while it was still beating and held it up for the whole world to see, like a sacrificial Peruvian llama.

"What do **YOU** want, Monica? Don't tell me what other people want from you. Is this what you want?" Peter asked earnestly.

"Yes…." came her sad reply as she quickly looked away. She couldn't stand to look into his penetrating gaze anymore. Peter stood up and looked at Monica defiantly biting his lip, not wanting to say any more. He exited the restaurant without waiting for his food, or saying goodbye, or even looking back once.

Peter spent another couple of days visiting each and every dot on his map where a possible tunnel entrance site could be planned and excavated. He was wrapping up his work, and he was really pleased to be finishing the project. Peter had also spent some time boxing up his soil and rock samples that he would ship back to California by a courier service. He would do some physical property testing on the samples in the lab to determine acidity, compaction, particle size analysis, density, conductivity, trace metals scans by ICP, and various other valuable tests. Peter knew he would need to do an exhaustive inorganic and organic chemistry testing program on the samples in his lab as well. He also needed to do hydrocarbon and contamination testing to do his due diligence for the Balboa Explorations. Upon completion of the testing, he would be able to send a final report to the Spanish consortium to complete the study.

Peter debated if he should tell Pablo and the Balboa Exploration group about the entrance below the restaurant and of his findings in the tunnel. Peter decided that for now he was just going to keep Monica's secret to himself. He didn't want to think about Monica at all. Every time he thought about her it hurt too much. He consciously had to quickly focus his thoughts on something else. It was just too painful to go there. Peter had made some really good maps of the tunnel from the restaurant entrance, and he had spent a lot of time in the evenings in his apartment categorizing all the artifacts and objects from the many pictures he had taken. He was amazed at the amount of information that he was putting together from his photographs and his memory of those incredible few minutes in the tunnel. Every time Peter scrolled through the pictures on his laptop he just couldn't believe it. They left him spellbound.

The bags were once again all packed and piled at the front entrance of his apartment waiting for a cab to the airport. Peter's landlady, Maria, stood with him talking about her new flowers that she had planted in the back of her house. They both watched as the little white cab pulled up to their front door. The little old women gave him the same Peruvian hug that he had received twice before only this time it was with more emotion and passion. She kissed him on one cheek and then on the other. Peter had to stoop so low for this exchange that he thought that he would fall over. He was going to miss Cusco and especially Peru, that was for sure. But, it was 7000 miles away from home, and that was just too far. He had come to love this very green, mountainous country, and especially its people that were so kind and loving. Peter half expected that Monica would show up to at least say good-bye and see him off. Besides Monica was the first person that he had met. It seemed only fitting somehow that she would be the last one he would see when he left. He knew that his landlady had phoned Monica and kept her up to date about Peter's whereabouts and travel plans. He had caught the little old lady talking to Monica a couple of times about him on the phone. Monica was being strong in her convictions and she didn't come. Peter didn't know if he even now trusted himself when it came to Monica. It was just as well. It was better this way.

Peter had been disappointed all day that Monica had not come to the apartment or to the airport. Peter had printed off a picture, and he wrote a short note on the back of it for Monica and left it in his room. He knew his landlady would give it to Monica. Now, he had a few hours to kill again in Lima as he waited for his international flight which didn't leave until around midnight. He had already checked his luggage in at the counter and he got his tickets and boarding passes all squared away.

All of a sudden, a thought came racing through his brain. "I don't have a picture of her," he exclaimed out loud. Several people standing around him quickly turned their attention to this handsome young American to see if he were speaking to them. Peter ran out the front door of the airport and hailed a cab. "Let's go to the Museum of Archeology. Please hurry," Peter instructed the cab driver. Peter, again spoke to the driver a half hour later as they pulled up to the museum. "Wait here, I'll be back quickly." Within moments, Peter was furiously taking pictures of the oil paintings of the Inca Princess, Lacoya Ines. A museum worker came running down the aisle waving his finger at him.

"No, you can't take any pictures, here!" the museum worker angrily confronted him. Peter put his camera away and pulled out an American twenty dollar bill, which quickly appeased the angry man.

Peter laughed inside, "Ah ha…. Now, I have you. I couldn't leave without you, don't you know. Peter said with one long last look at the paintings. "Thanks! Take me back to the airport, please!" Peter enthusiastically said to the cab driver as he dropped down into his seat. He had to laugh within himself when he was back in the cab, "I have you now, forever."

Chapter Notes – Chapter 17

The world famous ruins of Sacsahuaman are the second most photographed ruins in South America next to of course the ruins of Machu Pichu. They are a very impressive set of three lines of defense with each wall eighteen feet tall. Some of these colossal stones weigh upward of 400 tons and are a marvel to modern science how they were moved, carved, and put into place without our modern machinery of today. When the Spaniards arrived, the three observation towers and the tunnels were all still in place and serviceable. The conquistadors destroyed much of the complex using the stones for building their own cathedrals and palaces. Many wonderful things were destroyed looking for Inca gold and treasure over the next several centuries.

The Tomb of Francisco Pizarro resides in the Lima Cathedral in a chapel that bears the name of Francisco. The remains were brought back to this location in 1985 on the 450 year anniversary of the founding of Lima.

Chapter 18

Cusco Restaurant – Modern Day

Peter's landlady had let Monica into Peter's room. It still wasn't rented out, yet, because it had only been vacated the day before. She had come at once when the old lady had phoned and told her of a letter that Peter had left for her. Monica took the letter and sat down on the bed. She could almost smell, the handsome young American. She touched the patch quilt on the bed and caressed it. Oh, how she missed him. She suddenly realized that she did not even have a picture of him. Monica quickly looked around the room to see if Peter had left anything. The room was empty of anything except the simple furnishings that had been supplied. She had nothing of his, and all at once a terrible sadness gripped her heart. Monica took the large brown envelope that had her name on it and quickly opened it by just ripping the envelope apart. She couldn't believe how much blood her heart was pumping. She was more excited than she could ever remember, like a small child opening up a birthday present. She gasped at what she saw. Monica turned the picture over, and through tears that were freely flowing read the following note written in Peter's own handwriting:

My Dear Monica,

If we could only learn how to love from the example of your ancestors. The Princess was a peacemaker. Governor Francisco tried to protect her, her culture, and her temple to the day they died. They truly loved each other.

For Always, Peter

She turned the picture over again and gazed at it intently. The Spanish Conquistador was sitting on one throne chair and the Princess Lacoya Ines sat in the other. She hadn't noticed before that they were both looking at each other, deep into each others eyes. This photo was a good close up that showed clearly that they were holding hands with their fingers intertwined. It was beautiful. She started to cry uncontrollably, and just laid there staring at the photo. It was just too much for one person's heart to take.

Monica had just returned from Peter's apartment after retrieving the letter. She was running excitedly through the apartment looking for her mother everywhere. "Mother! Mother look at this picture and note," Monica screamed with joy. She was doing her little jumping up and down movement that Peter had thought was so endearing. She couldn't help it. "He **LOVES** me! He **LOVES** me!" Monica exploded. She flung the photograph at her Mother as she danced around her in circles. Eva Rodriguez picked up the piece of paper and she gazed at the photograph. Comprehension was dawning on Eva's face. The wrinkled lines on her brow smoothed, and her eyes filled with tears. She gasped, "I can't believe this. You actually saw them?"

"Yes, Mama, I told you we actually saw them. This letter means that he loves me, too, and that he will protect the ancient Inca secrets.

Mother it's a miracle. He loves me. I must go to him. Can we go to America and find him? Can we afford to go?" questioned Monica.

"Oh, Monica.....how wonderful this picture is. I can't believe you actually saw them. Oh, Monica, he is a special young man. And I can see that he loves you truly." The heart of Eva Rodriguez was quickly melting and she could see that she had been wrong about Peter.

"Well, mother, can we afford to go to America?" coaxed Monica earnestly.

Eva's simple response was, "we can't afford not to!"

Chapter Notes – Chapter 18

Lima, Peru is nearly 6000 miles away from New York City and approximately due north. California is more of a northwest direction. A direct airplane flight is usually eight to ten hours from the U.S. depending on the city of destination.

There are several probable entrance sites of the famous tunnels of
Cusco that surface at the Fortress of Sacsahuaman

Chapter 19

Martin Hacienda, California – Modern Day

Peter had now been home from Peru for the last two weeks. He had spent most of his time on the back of a horse in the foothills of the Sierra Nevadas on his family's ranch in Northern California. From his childhood he had loved to explore the canyons and hills looking for rocks and other interesting geological specimens. This was Peter's favorite world, the old home ranch. Good help was getting harder and harder to find on this huge ranch at any reasonable price. As usual Peter's father, Jose Martin, was short on wranglers this summer. Everyone still called Peter's father 'Don Jose' more out of respect for the old gentleman than for the Spanish tradition and class. Don Jose was sort of an oddity these days instead of being the high position of a 'Don' from days long since past, that no one cared about. Don Jose still dressed like a Spanish gentleman and still wore a beautifully embroidered sombrero whenever he went out doors. Peter loved his father tremendously, even though Peter thought that he should have been born two centuries earlier so that his dress and thought patterns would have matched that time period.

Peter did not like working with cattle or the other rigorous duties of the ranch hands. Last week when his father asked if Peter would like to join them on the summer work project to repair fence and look for mountain lions that were killing some new-borne calves, Peter just said, "sure, love to." Actually, Peter was still feeling a bit love sick, and this activity would be just what Peter needed to take his mind off his recent experiences in Peru. It was therapeutic for Peter. He got to ride around in the hills on his horse and just do what he loved most since he was a kid. Peter's father was old school and even though the work could have been done much easier and more efficiently with modern methods and equipment, they were stuck with the old ways and traditions. The ranch did not even own an SUV or quad. They did have two new pickup trucks, but they were rarely used. Horses were still used for transportation and to do the manual labor that needed to be done. Peter didn't care, it was a way of life and he loved it. He did not want to be the one in this long line of Martin landowners to make the changes necessary to modernize the business. Peter knew that the agricultural economics of the ranch would be substantially better if they made some changes. Unfortunately, Peter resisted the changes as much as his father did because they would also bring a change in the way of life that he had always known. It was quite a paradox actually, Peter on one hand had always been quite vocal about the family getting on board with the 21st century, and yet it was the 'old ways' he liked so much and the reason he returned as often as possible. Deep down he knew that he was just like his father in many ways, but he didn't want to admit it to himself let alone his father.

The problem for Peter lately in his strained relationship with his parents revolved around his current marital status. Being single at twenty-five years of age was not endearing him in the family circles. Peter had not made parents or grandparents happy at all with his choice of girlfriends either. Of course family traditions warranted a specific type of spouse for their eldest son and eventual heir to the family businesses and real estate properties, and future name sake for the Martin progeny. Peter actually hated these constant negative parental discussions regarding his dating activities. Shelley, his last girlfriend and his lab assistant at the university, had been the last one that was berated openly by a verbal barrage from his parents. Peter did not understand why they couldn't see the same wonderful qualities that she exhibited to him. Peter's relationship with his parents had gotten noticeably better with the news that Shelley was now engaged to someone else. These days Peter's thoughts kept returning to Peru and his last two months there. Now, Monica was the girl that was constantly on Peter's mind, but he had not seen any wisdom at all in letting his parents know anything about her. So, they did not even know that she existed let alone that Peter was in love with her. "Wow!" Peter whistled under his breath, "can that really be true. Am I really in love with a girl that lives six thousand miles away in Peru? How stupid is that?" Every evening when he slept outside under the stars in his sleeping bag he was haunted by her memory. By daybreak reality would always set in that it was crazy to worry about Monica at all. Peter needed to move on. He knew that going back to school next week would bring a new chapter to his life and help him to 'move on', to get his life back.

Peter had seen a few tracks, but he never actually saw a cougar. He always seemed to be a day or two behind the most recent kill. Even though the summer was almost over the hills had received more rain this summer than ever in recent memory. So, correspondingly, the hills had responded with a verdant green carpet that was unusual for this time of year. The cattle were also responding with growth rates that were really impressive. Soon the hot summer days would be over and the normal cooler rainy periods of fall would continue this green and beautiful scenery. Peter would actually have enjoyed the upcoming cattle roundup this year. He would have to miss the annual tradition because he would be back at his university. There would be another potential very awkward situation brewing on the horizon next week with Shelley. She had recently got engaged while Peter was working in Peru during the summer. Shelley was still committed to be his lab assistant for the coming semester at Cal Berkley. It was Peter's last term coming up before finishing his doctorate in geology and graduating in December. His relationship was going to be difficult with Shelley. Peter knew he still cared for her. In the back of his mind, though, Peter wondered if he shouldn't stay home this term on the ranch where it was safe, and avoid this upcoming disaster. Shelley had broken it off to go back to an old boyfriend from her hometown of Las Vegas. Peter couldn't help wondering how committed she would be to this fiancé or would he still have a chance to get back together with her once they were working side by side again. On the other hand this whole concept would not make his parents very happy. They were absolutely ecstatic when they heard the news that Shelley had broken it off with Peter.

It was not Shelley though that haunted Peter, and caused him the sleepless nights, it was the beautiful Peruvian girl, Monica. Peter could not help himself; he was addicted. Each night after supper he retired to his room early instead of going out with his friends. Peter had to scroll through the digital photographs that he had taken of the secret Tunnels of Cusco and of course the museum murals. Peter had spent most of his time at home these two weeks analyzing the photos. He had categorized and inventoried the treasure as best he could from his memory with the help of digital pictures. Peter had also tried to analyze the depth and structure of the tunnel itself, and map it out to the best of his ability. He knew at some point he would have to return to Peru and the incredible secret tunnels under the Incan capital city of Cusco. At the end of each of these sessions before bed, Peter would have to again gaze at the photos of the Inca Princess, Lacoya Ines. The princess looked exactly like his Incan beauty, Monica. And as it turned out it was for good reason. Lacoya Ines was the wife of the famous Conqueror of Peru, Francisco Pizarro. She was also the great-great-great-great-great-great-grandmother of Peter's very own Monica. It was an obsession really. Peter had no control over himself. The addiction was very real. Every night he had to look at the pictures and see her again and again. He had to keep the memory alive, somehow, because it already seemed like a long ago dream.

Peter had made a promise to her. He could not tell the world about their discovery. Peter had promised to keep their experience of exploring one of the tunnels a secret. It was going to be a huge problem for him. Tomorrow he would return to Berkley, and the University of California to finish his doctorate in geology. Peter knew that he must report his findings to his graduate professor and write up a paper for the dean of the College of Geology about the summer project. The Spanish consortium, Balboa Explorations, had teamed up with the university to do a Ground Penetrating Radar study of the City of Cusco. It had long been rumored that there were ancient tunnels under the city where the Incans had hidden most of their golden treasures before the Spanish Conquistadors arrived in their Incan capital city in 1533. Balboa Explorations finally had proof of the existence of the tunnel network, but couldn't get permission to enter or find the openings of the tunnels. No one was willing to give them permission to dig up the streets for what most considered just ancient sewer and irrigation canals. Only Peter had remained behind to finish the project and that is when Monica and Peter had made their discovery. He was still uncertain why he had to keep it a secret, and why they couldn't shout the news from the rooftops and make it known to the world. It had something to do with Monica's ancient Incan beliefs and a Sacred Quipu that was supposed to be guarded with the keeper's life. "What would it matter, anyway, he would never see Monica, again, so why worry," Peter thought. "Anyway, someday it wouldn't matter anymore. Balboa Explorations would make their tunnel finding public to the world and all of these secrets and promises would have no value anymore." Peter had to look one more time and scroll through again the museum pictures of Lacoya Ines. He was tired, exhausted actually. His father, Don Jose, was the hardest working man he had ever known and he expected everyone else on the ranch to work just as hard. No wonder he was so tired. Tomorrow he would be back at Berkley. Maybe Peter could sleep on it some more, and decide tomorrow exactly how much he could tell the university people without breaking his word and violating his covenant.

Chapter Notes – Chapter 19

There are still ranches in California of old Mexican heritage. These estates were given away to Spanish gentlemen centuries ago by the King of Spain. Many Spanish haciendas still exist in California, today.

Picture inside the temple complex of the walls of the Temple of
Koricancha which had the legendary 700 panels of pure
gold attached to them.

Chapter 20

San Francisco Airport – One Week Later

"Mother, are you sure we are doing the right thing?" queried Monica as they stood at the baggage carousel. Monica and her mother had just arrived from Peru via Bogotá and then Los Angeles a half hour ago. It was quite an adventure for the two of them, because neither woman had ever been to the United States let alone out of the country of Peru.

"Don't forget that this was your idea, Monica," Eva Rodriguez chuckled. "You're not backing out, now are you? You don't have cold feet do you?" Eva Rodriguez was laughing now and having a good time with the whole situation.

"Well, I just didn't think you'd take me up on it. And besides, Mom, this is really a dumb idea. Maybe Peter doesn't love me, this could be a very awkward and uncomfortable experience," moaned Monica. "We should have phoned him, or written him, or something. We can't just show up at his ranch and knock on the door of the hacienda and say, 'Is Peter home,' can we?" Now, the anxiety was starting to kick in and

Monica realized how vulnerable her position was. She was starting to get in panic mode. "Mom, let's just go back! Peter doesn't even need to know that we came to the airport." Monica beseeched her Mother with her favorite puppy-dog expression.

"Now Monica, you need to stay the course, here. We have come a long way to find out what this young man is thinking. You want to find out if he loves you. I want to find out who he has told about the secret tunnels and if he will keep his word," cautioned Eva.

"Mother, so you do have ulterior motives and feelings about Peter!" exclaimed Monica.

"Yes, of course, I want to find out just what this young man is made of, and if he is worthy of marrying my only daughter. And, yes, I do think he is too handsome for you to make a legitimate educated decision about on your own. So, I have come along on this escapade to assess the situation and give you vital grounded information," said Eva with as straight a face and sober expression as possible.

"Oh, Mother....you're impossible," sighed Monica. "You're going to be no help at all. We don't know where he lives or how to get there. We don't even know if he will be home. We don't have his phone number. We don't know if he even wants to see me let alone come for a visit. We don't...."

"Hush, now, Monica....you're starting to even give me cold feet. Let's just start with what you do know. You know that the ranch is just outside of Sacramento. You know that his last name is Martin and that the ranch has been in the family for generations. You know that he still goes home and lives there with his folks when he is not at school. So, we go to Sacramento and start from there. We'll find a bus that can take us there to the ranch. Monica, life is about what you know….not about what you don't know. Besides, I am sure that he will be happy to see you." Eva consoled her daughter with a more serious tone. "Besides, this might be fun!"

It was beginning to be late afternoon, and the shadows from the large cottonwood trees that lined the dusty lane cooled the approach to the ranch house. A local bus had dropped Monica and her mother by the highway turnoff from Sacramento. It had been a long day. They were tired and it had been too long of a day to lug their heavy suitcases up the cobblestone way. They could see off in the distance the large trees that framed the old Spanish hacienda and gave the mansion a very picturesque look. It had not been hard to find this beautiful place. Everyone seemed to know where the Martin ranch was and it was even listed in the Sacramento tourist guides. "Need some help?" A voice from behind Monica and Eva startled them. A young very tall boy dressed in Levi's and a plaid shirt stepped out from behind an old Oak and strode up to the two ladies. He was obviously one of the cowhands employed at the ranch. "My name's Andrew Sommers, but most people just call me Andy around here," he continued. "Are you going up to the house? I'll go fetch a truck."

The wrangler was off running at full speed down the lane and yelling, "stay right there. I'll be right back," over his shoulder without even looking back. Monica and her mother just stood there gaping. They never even had a chance to say a word The two ladies just dropped their bags and stared after the young man.

"Well, I just hope we get as good a reception from the rest of the Martin family," said Eva dryly as she sat down on her largest suitcase. They did not have to wait long. Andy was back within five minutes with a new white Chevy Sierra 4x4 pickup with the words, 'Martin Ranch' stenciled on the sides. Seconds later, Andy had the bags in the back, and with a very large grin stood at the passenger side door. He opened it with a great flair for the two women, and quickly helped them step up inside. Before she knew it, Monica stood outside the two large wooden doors that designated the front entrance to the massive hacienda.

"Oh, Mother! I don't know if I can do it....Maybe we should turn around and go home!" Monica started to panic all over again. Eva Rodriguez did not say anything, but just took three steps up to the door and pounded loudly several times.

"Oh, don't worry about that, just go right in!" Andy said enthusiastically as he got up to the front steps with the last of the bags. Andy opened the old antique oak door and motioned for them to enter. "Just stay right here in the lobby and I'll go get Don Jose." In an instant Andy disappeared down one of the long hallways that emanated from the foyer. The floor was all a polished tile with some sort of Aztec design, and the walls were a brilliantly white washed plaster over adobe brick. The ceiling beams were lacquered and opened to the next floor. In the center of the foyer was a huge wagon wheel chandelier light giving the whole interior a very rustic traditional Mexican ranch design. Monica had never seen anything so authentically Western. Somehow it felt friendly and warm, it wasn't what she had imagined or even dreamed about. From a room far down the hallway a voice came bellowing towards Monica and Eva. They could hear Don Jose say, "Andy, we aren't expecting any relatives for a visit. Who are they? Did they tell you their names?"

"Sorry, Don Jose, in all of the excitement I forgot to ask them their names or why they were here," pleaded Andy.

"Okay, okay, show them into the library, and I'll be right there," Don Jose spoke in a loud bass voice that echoed down the hall.

"Thank you, Hefe!! Good afternoon, Senor," called Andy.

"Ladies....Please come right this way to the library. Don Jose, will be with you in just a moment. I'll take care of your suitcases. We weren't expecting any visitors, sorry!" said Andy apologetically. "Please be seated."

"Good afternoon, ladies, my name is Don Jose. How may I be of service to you?" Don Jose spoke cautiously as he bowed deeply. He was visually astonished with the appearance of these beautiful Spanish women who he had never seen before. "My wife, Isabela, is away in town shopping this afternoon. Did you come to see her?" said Don Jose in his cordial greeting.

"Don Jose, it is nice to meet you," Monica spoke slowly so as to not betray her Peruvian Spanish accent too noticeably. "I am Monica Rodriguez, and this is my mother Eva Rodriguez. We have come here from Cusco, Peru, to find my friend, Peter Martin. Is he here?" asked Monica nervously.

"Peter, my son Peter....you are looking for Peter. No, uh, Peter has gone back to school since last week," stammered Don Jose.

"Oh, I am sorry, then that we have bothered you, Senor. Do you have a phone number and Peter's address where we can reach him at his university? We will go back to Sacramento and give him a call. Thank you for your trouble Don Jose."

"No....I will not give you anything until you tell me a little more, and how you know Peter." A soft smile was emerging on this old weathered gentleman and he was actually getting some amusement out of Monica's uncomfortable situation. Eva Rodriguez just sat there not saying a word in her overstuffed chair with her eyes twinkling and getting lots of satisfaction from this conversation as well

Chapter Notes – Chapter 20

No notes

Picture of a llama on the Peruvian hillsides around Cusco

Chapter 21

University of California, Berkley – Later that night

"Peter, guess who we had come to visit us today?" asked Isabela Martin for the third time.

"Oh, I don't know. Just tell me, okay. I don't have time to play games on the telephone tonight. I have an important paper due tomorrow and a lab class to prepare for. I can't play this game anymore." Peter said in a disinterested tone.

"Oh, Peter come on…just one more try, one more guess! I told you a clue, two ladies that you know. Come on I'll give you one more guess, who do you think they are?"
coaxed Isabela Martin, again.

"Mom, I give up. Just tell me who they are so we can get on with this conversation, and so I can get back to work." Peter was annoyed now and wanted to just get back to writing his paper that was due tomorrow and he still had a lot of work to do on it. Peter knew he would be up for several hours finishing the project. This phone call was going to limit each precious minute of sleep that he would eventually receive after a late night of studying.

"Oh, alright…but you remember that I've told you many times that you are not any fun at all. All I wanted was to have a little enjoyment with my only son. This is such exciting news. It's the best thing that has happened around the hacienda for months. I'm just so thrilled. Your father is so extremely pleased that he is beside himself, too. They're wonderful… I'm so happy!" gushed Isabela.

"Mom!!!...Mom, quit already, I give up! Just tell me the news, please. I'm listening," answered Peter. Peter could feel an anger stirring deep in his soul towards his mother that had never happened before. This is the one woman that he could definitely say that he truly loved. A glimmer of recognition came across his face and he decided he needed a change of tactic here, a silent treatment. "Okay, I'm waiting…," was all he said. Then there was dead silence for a few moments.

"Monica Rodriguez and her mother, Eva, are here at the ranch with us! They arrived at the hacienda from Peru this afternoon!"

"Who?...What?..." Peter gasped. "Are you sure?...Why would they come to the ranch…to California?" stammered Peter as the realization of the situation settled into his brain.

"Yes, isn't it exciting. We are so happy….and she is so beautiful. Peter you must come home at once. They were expecting to see you here," Peter's mother said anxiously.

"No, mother, it is Wednesday night, and I have school tomorrow. I can't, it is really important to me. Besides, what do they want, why did they come here?" Peter tried to disguise his emotions and his own excitement.

"Peter you didn't tell me you had a new girlfriend? She is wonderful and your father and I are enchanted with her. We have asked them to stay with us here at the hacienda," soothed Isabela Martin in a teasing attitude. Isabela Martin was your typical metteling and yet loving middle-age mother that was too protective of her offspring. Yet, she was totally in love with her children.

"What!... They are going to stay at the ranch? Mom, she is **not** my girlfriend. Well we are friends, but I never thought she would ever come to California. I never thought I would ever see her again. Why did they come here?" Peter again asked.

"Yes, Peter isn't that wonderful...come home immediately, okay?" said Isabela anxiously.

"No!...I can't come home now. Oh, Mother what have you gotten me into? Tell them to go home. I have to go....Good night!" Peter hung up the phone quickly before his mother could respond again. He had so much to do, and now this! How was he going to be able to concentrate on his school work tonight, now with this problem?

It had now been two days since Isabela Martin had talked to her son, Peter, on the phone and told him that Monica had arrived from Cusco. The Martins had had a very memorable time playing the good hosts and had really enjoyed entertaining Monica and her Mother. Monica

181

had resisted at first the genuine friendship and hospitality offered by the Martins. Eva had come to her aid and accepted their kind offer to stay a few days at the ranch until Peter could come home. Don Jose had embraced the opportunity to be the gracious host and to take the ladies horseback riding and on little drives everyday until he had exhausted every square acre of the massive ranch. The Martins also enjoyed showing the Rodriguez women around Sacramento and took them shopping. They were having more fun than Monica and Eva. Isabela had phoned Peter each night, and finally Peter had capitulated. "Okay!... Okay!...Mom, we've been talking about this for a half hour already. I don't want to come home. There you have it. I think she's in love with me and I don't know what to do about it. She scares me! I'd prefer to just stay here at school. I am very busy, and she just confuses me. I would just get in the middle of a difficult situation if I came home," said Peter with a lot of feeling.

"Oh, Peter, I can see what you mean….we have only known Monica for a couple of days, and we already love her, too. She's fantastic! Peter you have to come home. I didn't want to tell you, but I have organized a huge party for them on Saturday night. You have to come home. You will embarrass your father and I if you do not come. Everyone is expecting you to be here for this surprise party. I love you, Peter. You have to come," begged Peter's mother.

"Okay, I'll come home for the weekend. But, you have to try and help me through this. I am in a bad situation, here. Will you promise me that you will help me and not cause me more problems with Monica, Mother?"

Peter knew that this weekend was going to be a turning point in his life somehow. It would end up being forever the kind of decision making part of your life that decided how the rest of your mortal existence turned out. Things had not gone well with Shelley, Peter's old girlfriend. Peter took her out to dinner once at his insistence, and against her better judgment. The spark or fire from their previous relationship was now cold. Peter could feel it acutely. How strange to have loved someone so much and now to see and feel that love to have vanished away. He had resolved some issues with her that would make working with Shelley bearable this semester. That was good, at least they would be friends and could work together. Peter really longed for more, she was so beautiful and fun. Now, all he could do was admire her at a distance. Shelley was thoroughly committed to her engagement and it was not going to change. Driving the two hours out to the ranch was a good time and therapeutic for Peter. He was away from the pressures of his responsibilities at the university and he was having the opportunity to think his way through some important problems. Peter had now put his relationship with Shelley aside, and closed that chapter of his life. As he drove down the freeway another girl was now haunting all the corners of his brain. Peter tried to think of all the reasons why Monica might have come to America. For weeks he had tried to forget her. That wasn't going to happen, especially now that she had come to California to pursue him on his own turf. Could he just be friends with Monica or had their relationship blossomed into something larger, something out of control? It was all giving Peter's head a buzz, even a throbbing headache. The main question was: 'Did he love her?'

Peter shook his head violently, and rotated his head back and forth and around to relieve the strain from driving. "I've got to concentrate and focus on the things that I want to get accomplished while we are together. I have so many questions from my analysis of the tunnel," Peter said to himself. "Monica and her mother no doubt know some of the answers that I am looking for about the treasure. I wonder if I can get them to cooperate with me if I devise a good plan that will work for everyone."

Peter had actually written down a list of questions that he had for Monica and her mother. He intended to sit down with the both of them and ask them some frank straight forward questions about the tunnel and what they knew from their Sacred Quipu. Peter knew it wasn't going to be easy to get the answers especially from Eva Rodriguez. Somehow, he needed to get Monica's mother on his side. Eva had warmed up to him in their restaurant and he knew that the problems had more to do with her ancient Inca roots and religious commitments than her hatred of him personally. So, Peter needed to change his approach and not make her feel threatened by him or his research. A private meeting with them at the ranch was what Peter needed. Asking all the right questions might put him back in good standing with the mother. He must have courage. Quite frankly Eva scared him immensely. That thought was interesting to Peter because there was nothing about Monica's mother that was really scary. It must be a knowledge that he was insecure in his relationship with her daughter that created the rift between them. The whole thing was mind boggling to Peter. At last he came to the realization that he had to change his thinking process and concentrate on what he was going to say in this all important meeting. For the next hour as he drove to the hacienda, Peter tried to focus on the different points that he needed to get across and how he might best address them to his Peruvian guests. Analyzing this thing out like a good scientist was giving Peter more and more confidence the closer he got to home.

"Hi, you look gorgeous as usual! How was your trip to California? What do you think of my country?" Peter rattled off several memorized sentences before Monica had a chance to say a word. Peter was actually stunned. She did look even more fantastic than he had remembered her from his dreams. It was a good thing that he had practiced his lines.

"Hi, well it's good to see you, too." Monica looked around the room nervously at all the people watching and witnessing this amusing event. The great room at the hacienda was crowded with Peter's parents, Eva Rodriguez, a couple of cleaning ladies, their cook, and just about every cowhand that Don Jose had currently on the ranch payroll and even a few extra people that had come to see this historical meeting. It looked like everyone had come to see the blessed event and see the look on Peter's face when he finally waltzed into the hacienda late that Friday night. Peter approached the two visitors and quickly offered his hand to Eva Rodriguez and then Monica. That moment was a little strange and awkward. No Peruvian hug and no kiss for either side of his cheek. An instantaneous flash came through his brain saying that he should someday analyze the difference in their two cultures and the greetings between the two peoples. Monica leaned over to Peter and said softly, "Peter can we go somewhere to talk. I'm a little self conscience about sharing things with everyone here."

"Sure we can." Peter grinned at Monica. "Hi, Mom and Dad, and all the rest of you that have come here tonight to embarrass me in front of Monica, nice to see you all! I hope you have a good time at your little gathering here tonight, at my expense. Remember that Saturday is still a work day around here tomorrow, and that my father doesn't give anyone a day off unless it is Sunday," Peter said with a laugh. With a loud voice and almost shouting Peter said, "Monica and I are now going out into the courtyard to talk." They all giggled and laughed as Peter took Monica's hand and led her out of the room and down the hallway. The Martin hacienda was a traditional Spanish building with a huge open air courtyard or garden in the middle of the building on the bottom floor. This was Peter's favorite place to go in his home. It had a huge fountain in the center of the square plaza with a ceramic tiled floor. The fountain was surrounded by pathways in and out of various plantings of flowers and shrubbery. On either side of the main fountain there were two cement benches. They were not unlike a special bench in another garden in another world that now seemed like a long ago dream.

"So, did you miss me?" giggled Monica at her first opportunity to say something when they sat down. That was classic 'Monica'; she always took the offensive and was totally brutally honest. It always put Peter on the defensive and made him a little self conscience around her. But this time Peter was ready and had been practicing his lines.

"Sure, I missed you…like the measles, chicken pox, or the flu or something. You're like a disease that I can't get rid of !" Peter teased. I thought I was over you and now I've caught you again. Seriously, I tried to forget you these past couple of weeks, and I was doing a good job of it, and then here you go again and show up at my **HOUSE!**"

"Oh, Peter," Monica pouted with her protruding lip act that annoyed Peter. "I knew that you loved me and I just had to see you….so that you wouldn't forget me."

The garden area was only lit by three tall lamps placed in the perimeter. All at once Peter wished that they had better lighting so he could see her features more clearly. Peter turned to look deep into her eyes and moved closer. "How can I forget you when every time I turn around, you are there....standing in front of me!" Peter put his arm around her and drew her to him and kissed her as if he'd never kissed her before.

The next morning the smells of the kitchen were wafting through the whole house. Isabela Martin was busily making pancakes for breakfast which was her usual routine for a Saturday morning. Six o'clock came early in the Martin ranch, and Don Jose had gone out to check on the stock. He also was checking on the oranges and grapefruit to see when they would be ready to harvest. The cook usually had the weekends off and so the kitchen was Isabela's domain and she loved the weekends. The whole staff needed to be back that evening to help with the big party that the Martins were throwing for their new guests. Peter sat on his kitchen stool that he had had since he was a child watching her work. Peter was nursing a cup of hot chocolate and listening to his mother recount what was happening on the ranch. This morning however, Isabela, was as excited as a little school girl trying to pry out of her oldest son any morsel of information that she could glean from him. "Peter, Monica is just marvelous, we love her. What do you think about her?"

"Oh, I don't know Mom. She's a girl I met in Peru while I was doing the geological survey for the university. But, you already know all of that," responded Peter drowsily.

"Yes, but do you love her? Are you going to marry her? Your father and I have both talked about it and we heartily approve."

"Mom, will you quite prying already. It's not like that. We are just friends and had to work together on the project. I forgot that I had

187

invited her here to California for a visit. Actually, I never thought that she would take me up on the offer, come to think of it. Here she is. What can I say?"

"But, Peter isn't this the same girl that the state department told us was kidnapped with you by the terrorists?" questioned Isabela.

"Sure she is, but the terrorists had us tied up in different cabins. I did help her escape with me, but that's all. Don't make it anymore than it is." These half-truths that Peter was telling his mother made him uncomfortable, but he knew he couldn't tell her the whole truth right now. Maybe sometime in the future then he could, but for now he needed to keep things simple.

"Peter there is more to this than what you're saying, I know there is. Come on you can tell your own mother," begged Isabela Martin.

"No, Mom, I promise you that we are just friends. Besides, remember that I am trying to get back together with Shelley. We went out just the other day." Peter lied, trying to defuse the conversation and annoy his mother at the same time.

"What! You can't be serious, Peter. She can't even speak Spanish. We don't like her. I can't believe that you are still interested in her. Besides we thought that she was engaged to that young man from Las Vegas. Why can't you see how wonderful Monica is? Your father just can't stop talking about her." Isabela Martin was now all charged up and incensed with the tauntings of her only son. Somehow, she knew deep down inside that Peter was just toying with her and not telling her the truth.

"Oh, mother, you're impossible! I'm going to go out and see what dad's doing," said Peter as he put down his finished cup of coco. "I need some fresh air anyway. You're way too intense."

The festive lantern lights had been taken out of storage. The hacienda was decorated exquisitely, as never before at least in this century. The whole Martin family and all the farm personnel had spent the day in preparation for this event. A half of a beef was being cooked in the Bar-B-Q pit and a truck load of groceries was being prepared for the feast. It was going to be the biggest party that the ranch had ever done. Peter's grandparents were cutting their holidays short in Mexico City and flying back this afternoon for their fiesta. Don Jose drove into Sacramento to pick them up at the airport. Peter had actually had fun helping Monica put up the decorations and string up the lights. "So, I can't believe that you are forced to help me do all this work for *your* party," sighed Peter.

"Oh, it's fun, Peter, I want to help! Besides it lets me have a chance to work along side of you just like we did in Peru!" teased Monica.

"Ahhh, Peru….yea, I can't forget about Peru. Monica, why did you come here? I never thought I would see you again. Why are you here?" asked Peter again.

"Because I missed you, silly, I told you that already," giggled Monica. "Man, are you ever serious, today!" she said with a raised eyebrow.

"Yes, seriously, Monica, I need to have a meeting with you and your mother after the party tonight, okay?" Peter said gravely.

"Okay afterwards we can, but seriously, don't you want to know what I am wearing to the party, tonight? You're mother and I picked it out in Sacramento, yesterday. I can't wait. Do you want me to model it for you early, right now?"

"No, we have work to do. Whatever, you wear will be stunning. You're already distracting me big time, and we're way behind schedule. We're never going to be finished on time. So, you better focus on the job or I'm going to fire you and finish it on my own, thank you very much," Peter laughed feigning unhappiness.

The food, mariachi band, the lights and decorations, had all been perfectly prepared. "This is going to be the best night of our lives, isn't it, Peter?" Monica said coyly.

Peter just shrugged his shoulders and didn't answer, but Monica could see that he was thinking hard about something. "What did you want to talk to me and my mother about, tonight?" Monica said a little sheepishly.

"Oh, it's something important, something that I've been working on. We'll talk about it later, after the dance," that was all that Peter could say.

Chapter Notes – Chapter 21

Even though the most famous treasure in the history of Peru is the ransom, Atahualpa's treasure in Cajamarca of one room of Gold and two rooms of silver, piled as high as he could reach. This was undoubtedly not as large a dispersal of treasure as the one accumulated and dispersed in Cusco. The first large dispersal treasure or ransom presumably came mostly from the northern kingdom of Quito which was the homeland of Atahualpa. King Huascar was alive and controlled the capital of Peru, Cusco, for much of the imprisonment and so this treasure would not have been available to him. The largest dispersal and amount of treasure was found in Cusco. It was a treasure and a city, Eldorado, that Pizarro and Almagro would fight over for years, and eventually it would tear their one-time partnership and friendship apart. It finally cost Diego de Almagro his life in a civil war between the conquistadors. Almagro the younger would then murder the governor, Francisco Pizarro, years later in revenge for the treasure that had eluded both father and son.

The Chapel of Francisco Pizarro in Lima, Peru

Chapter 22

Martin Ranch – Present Day

The fiesta party at the Martin Ranch was the best that anyone could ever remember. Monica got a chance to finally meet many of the Martin family. Peter's grandparents were very gracious, and somehow Monica had felt like they had been tutored a head of time, that this was Peter's new girlfriend and that they were very serious. Peter had two younger sisters both of whom were not living at home anymore. The older of Peter's sisters, Patricia, was already married and living and working in Sacramento. Peter's youngest sister, Deanna, was in her first year of university at UCLA and living on campus in Los Angeles. Both sisters burst into Monica's bedroom while she was dressing for the party. They wanted to know everything that was going on. They talked like little school girls for an hour telling Monica everything they could remember about their childhood with their older brother, Peter. It was really embarrassing to be getting all of this attention. Monica couldn't help but fall in love with these two would-be sisters. She had never had a sister, and she relished the thought of finally getting the opportunity to have something that she had missed out on her whole life.

They asked Monica a lot of questions, everything from if they'd kissed to if they were going to get married. The two sisters offered lots of advice about Peter, what he liked and what he didn't like. They wanted to know what she took at university, and what was her job like. Did she have any trouble learning English, and how did she like America, were all questions that needed to be answered for the sisters. Neither one had ever met a girlfriend of Peter's since high school, anyway. Monica was exhausted, and the evening hadn't even started, yet. She was going to be late because she wasn't dressed or ready at all. After Patricia and Deanna had left her room, Monica just collapsed on the bed and closed her eyes. Was Peter really in love with her or was it just Monica's fantasy. She knew that she was crazy in love with this young handsome American no matter what reservations that her mother had. Monica opened her eyes and stared at the ceiling. "Why does Peter want to have a meeting with Mom and I? I wonder if he is going to propose to me, tonight! No, it can't be. It is too early. He is not ready for that, yet." The thoughts were racing through her mind. "Am I ready to get married? What will I say, if he asks me tonight? Monica, of course you will say, 'yes' won't you? Maybe, he will take me out into the garden courtyard again, like last night." Monica seemed to be talking out loud, instead of just having the thoughts flow through her; she was actually speaking them audibly. "Monica, pull yourself together. This is an important night in your life. You've got to get ready," a voice came into her conscience. At once she remembered what she had been waiting for these two days and Monica leaped off the bed and ran to the closet to get out her new dress.

As Monica came down the stairs from the second floor into the Great Room she could see that Peter's jaw had become unhinged and it gaped open. Monica had had that effect on him before, but this time he was stammering and finally speechless. Peter was magnificently dressed in a dark suit that had a western fit and design to it. It was accented with a bright green cummerbund. The guests were all richly attired in their finest. Monica's mother beamed all over when the grandparents looked up the stairs at her and whispered their approval to Eva Rodriguez. Monica had loved this dress from the first moment that she had seen it in the fancy Mexican boutique with Isabela Martin. It was an off-white full length satin gown with a very Mexican frilly fringe on the hem, sleeves and around the neckline. It was simply the most beautiful and expensive dress that Monica had ever seen. At just under one thousand dollars U.S. it was also certainly out of any price range that Monica or her mother could hope to entertain. Isabela Martin had seen Monica's face plummet when she glimpsed the amount on the price tag. Monica slowly put it back on the rack and then started to look at some of the other dresses. At once Isabela walked up to the rack of dresses and took the special dress in her hands and pressed it up against Monica. "I think maybe we should try this one on, don't you think?" smiled Isabela.

"Oh, no, I couldn't. It is way too much money; we can't possibly pay for it. I'll look for something else," Monica said frankly with some embarrassment.

"I'm sorry. What did you say? Who is taking *who* shopping? I invited you and your mother to come to Sacramento today with me to go shopping. That means that here in America I am paying for this dress. Besides I want to buy you a gift for you to remember your stay with us," Isabela stated firmly. "Now, get in there and try it on, please!"

"I can't accept such a gift, it is way too expensive," gushed Monica about to cry.

"Isabela…Monica is right," continued Eva Rodriguez. "We are already indebted to you and your husband for your hospitality and cannot repay all of your kindness."

"Hush now, the both of you. I have been waiting twenty-five years to buy something for my new daughter-in-law!" Eva was startled and Monica put her hand to her mouth, and was gasping for air. "I know, I know you are just friends says Peter. But, I have a feeling that it is more than that and I am so excited that I can't stand it. So, please get in there and try it on. Hurry now…." Isabela laughed at the expressions on their faces.

So, here she stood on the stairs in the ballroom on the most important night of her life in a dress that she couldn't afford, looking into the face of the most handsome guy in the world. Monica knew that she loved this new dress almost as much as the young man in front of her. Monica waited while Peter escorted her out onto the dance floor. The band was playing a slow song and Peter held her close and tightly. Finally, Peter was able to speak. "Wow, I've never seen that pretty dress before. You look amazing."

"Thanks, your mother bought it for me. Do you like it?" teased Monica

"Sure, it's beautiful. My mom's always got good taste, but I hope that you guys aren't getting too friendly. She doesn't know when to quit and she is going to drive me crazy," drawled Peter.

"Oh, Peter, she is just having so much fun, let her enjoy it," giggled Monica.

They started a second dance and with all the spinning and whirling Monica couldn't talk anymore, but was just content to watch Peter as he kept a steady gaze on her and her new dress. The dance was suspended at the call for supper. Everyone hurried to their seats. Monica had been looking forward to this part of the day ever since Isabela Martin had made the announcement about the party. Monica and her mother had sampled a lot of the American dishes during their stay and now maybe some real authentic Mexican food would be added to their gastronomical experience. Being in the restaurant business had made them keenly aware of new ways of how the food was prepared and served, here in the United States.

After the spectacular dinner Monica seemed to be asked to dance by every available young man in the room. Even Andrew Sommers, the helpful young cowhand had courageously asked Monica to dance. In the mean time Peter danced with his mother and several times with his sisters. Monica could see by the look on his face that he was not very happy about the apparent conspiracy to keep them apart. Monica thought she noticed a reddening in the face and jealousy when the last young man asked her to dance, and finally Peter boiled over. "Okay, you guys have had your little fun and I appreciate you all trying to show my friend, Monica, a good time, but enough is enough. It is my turn to dance with Monica…the rest of you…Take a hike!" warned Peter in a loud voice. Now, it was Monica's turn to be embarrassed as Peter grabbed her hand and took her out onto the dance floor.

The evening had ended way too soon. Monica stood next to Peter in the foyer near the front door saying good bye to the last of the guests. This was the moment that Monica was looking forward to and a little bit nervous about. This was the moment that Peter had been dreading. He was apprehensive and was uncertain about himself even though he had practiced the whole thing out in his mind several times. "Monica, can I speak with you and your mother in the library for a few minutes?" Peter whispered.

"Sure," was all that Monica could think of to say. Monica felt the touch of Peter's hand as he took it to lead her down the wide hallway with her mother following behind them. The library room had simple, but elegant furnishings. In the middle of the room was a long Mahogany table that was brightly polished with chairs positioned all around it. There were also two sofas and two recliner chairs with reading lamp tables. All around the room perimeter were book cases filled with hard-bound books. Some of the books looked new and some looked like extremely old leather-bound manuscripts. A nice adequate but rustic wagon wheel chandelier hung in the center of the room over the table. Monica waited as Peter offered her mother and then her a place to sit on one of the chairs at the table. He was trying to be a true gentleman by helping to seat each one in turn. Monica could see that this little gesture of chivalry and manhood had impressed her mother and was going to set the mood very well for their meeting.

Peter quickly stepped back to the library door and locked it from the inside. "There, hopefully, no one will bother us," smiled Peter. "Thank you for giving me a few minutes. I know I am treading on thin ice here, but I want to ask you a few questions about the tunnels of Cusco and the Sacred Quipu that you guard for your people!" Peter went directly to his lap top and video projector on top of the table. "I have a list of questions that I have prepared and that I want to ask you. But first, I want to show you a photo presentation of the digital photos that I took during our exploration of the tunnel under your restaurant." Monica suddenly felt a cold chill, and then her heart sink, and a terrible gloom seemed to hang over her. This isn't what she had expected at all. Peter walked to a nearby wall and pulled down a projection screen, and turned off the lights. He was so excited; anyone could see that he had been practicing this presentation for days, maybe weeks. The first series of photos were of the empty chamber, then another set showed the chamber that was full of animals and skeletons. The next set of photos projected were pictures that were taken of the treasure room. Peter showed Monica and her mother the research papers where Peter had categorized and documented every piece of treasure that Peter could analyze from the photos. The last few pictures were of the chamber with the golden thrones and presumably Francisco Pizarro and Lacoya Ines. Peter had given an enthusiastic narrative for ten minutes and commented on each new photo as it was displayed on the wall. Peter was oblivious to some little sniffles, coughs, and the quiet reserve of his guests. Eva Rodriguez was stunned; she couldn't say a word because she was so amazed at what she had seen. Peter walked back to the door and turned on the lights. He didn't even notice that Monica had been crying and her eyes were still red.

"Well, what do you think, Mrs. Rodriguez? I realize Monica has already seen the pictures and told you about them, but what do you think?" continued Peter in his same enthusiastic narrative tone as before.

"Peter, the pictures are truly amazing....I had no idea you could take that good of pictures in a dark tunnel," Eva whispered in a low voice, obviously very much aware and concerned about Monica's distress.

Peter pulled out a sheet of paper with writing on it and he picked it up and started reading. "Okay, I've written some questions down that I would like to discuss with you tonight. Number 1." Peter started reading the list: "Why is the embalmed body of Francisco Pizarro found here in the tunnel when his body is supposed to be entombed in his sanctuary in Lima? Number 2. Why is there so much treasure found here in the tunnel when the Spanish were supposed to have found it all and melted it down, when they originally looted the city in 1533? Number 3....."

Monica abruptly stood up in the middle of Peter's sentence. Peter looked up from the paper, and for the first time noticed that something was not quite right. "Peter, I am very tired. Please excuse me I think that I will go to my room and go to bed," Monica bravely said trying to disguise her voice and countenance.

"Monica is there something wrong?" Peter asked sympathetically. Peter just stood there astonished at the response that he was getting on such a wonderful presentation.

"No, nothing at all…," Monica turned immediately. She hurried and even ran to the door. Monica quickly unlocked it, and with her hand over her mouth, she started running down the hallway. She was crying now out loud; she opened her door and quickly slammed it closed behind her. Monica threw herself on her bed, and buried her face in her pillows, crying uncontrollably.

Peter was up early the next morning. He was distressed about how poorly things had gone the night before and he had tossed and turned all night. Peter could not remember a night when he had slept so little. He just couldn't get the whole thing out of his mind, and his stomach seemed to be tied up in knots. Peter found Eva Rodriguez standing by herself working in the large kitchen. Eva was obviously getting some breakfast put together for Monica that she was going to take back to her room. "Hi, Peter, we have decided to return to Peru today! Thank you for your kindness, and for your hospitality, Peter. We have truly enjoyed our stay here with you and your folks," she said matter-of-factly. It was a cordial enough conversation, and Peter was encouraged by her tone and that she was at least talking to him.

"Senora Rodriguez, it has been our pleasure. I guess I am confused and disappointed....I guess I don't know where I stand with you and Monica!" blurted out Peter.

"Well, I guess that is exactly why Monica and I wanted to come to California was to find out where she stood with you and what your intentions were. Last night, I think she found out where your heart resides and what your intentions really are," Eva responded. She was deliberately watching intently the expressions on Peter's face.

All of a sudden it was like a light bulb had come on, and Peter seemed to comprehend the significance of the previous evening. His face seemed to flash recognition of the problem, and an instant solution to it. "I have to go back to the university early in the morning. Could you please come with me to Berkley and visit with my supervising professor, Clayton Nelson. I would very much like you to meet him. My plan is very simple like I explained last night after Monica left. Did you give it some thought?" asked Peter.

"Yes, I think that is why we have decided to return to Peru," retorted Eva Rodriguez.

"Senora, I know I wasn't very sensitive to Monica last night and her feelings. I didn't realize that she was expecting something different from our meeting. I might have led her to believe something different earlier in the day. I do care for Monica, we are really good friends and someday maybe it will develop into something more. I will go see her immediately after I get through with my explanation. I hope that she will see me,"

Peter said passionately. For the first time Eva Rodriguez seemed to soften. Finally, it was the right thing to say and Peter could see that the problem needed to be dealt with from a different direction. "Senora Rodriguez, you are the modern day Inca Queen!" Eva's eyebrow turned up and she half smiled at Peter."

"How do you know that? I haven't even told Monica that I am the anointed Queen. Nobody knows that but the Incan Elders!" whispered Eva. She looked around the kitchen to make sure that no one else was within hearing distance.

"No one told me, I just guessed it somehow, and now I know that you and only you have the power to make these decisions. I just want to again ask permission to review these pictures and this discovery with Professor Nelson. We will omit the existence and keep sacred the knowledge of the burial chamber. We will just discuss the tunnel and the treasure chamber with him. Please this is all that I ask," begged Peter.

"Okay, okay….we will do it together!" Eva sighed slowly and quietly.

"Thanks…Oh thank you so very much. I must run quickly and see Monica." Peter was out of the kitchen in a flash and before Eva could say another word, he was gone.

Chapter Notes – Chapter 22

It is an interesting fact that Pizarro found more gold and treasure in his conquest of Peru than any other conqueror in the history of the world. Only about one fifth or twenty percent ever left Peru, the king's portion. It is true that Hernando Pizarro and a few others were able to return to Spain with some treasure. The rest remained in Peru, and presumably is mostly still hidden today. There is very little actual golden artifacts and treasure on display in museums and private collections at the present time. The whereabouts of the bulk of this treasure is still a mystery today.

Schematic Drawing of the Temple of Koricancha in Cusco, Peru

Chapter 23

Berkley, California – Present Day

Professor Nelson's office was a small cubicle on the third floor of the science building. The only real redeeming quality about this rather long narrow office was that it was situated on the Northwest corner and so it had two windows instead of just the normal one window office that was the common fare for Associate Professors. The office had two desks in a row on one side of the room and full bookshelves completely lined the other side of the room. The narrow walkway between the desks and bookshelves had always given Peter a sense of claustrophobia every time he came into this office. Professor Clayton Nelson was a twenty year veteran of this university and had still never actually become a department chairman or climbed significantly the political ranks of the college hierarchy. Professor Nelson was, however, academically brilliant and well-respected in his circle of associates. Peter revered Professor Nelson greatly. He didn't worship the ground that this rather short, skinny white-haired man walked on, but it was close. In fact, outside of his own father, Professor Nelson was probably Peter's favorite male role model in the whole world.

Peter introduced Monica and her mother to the elderly scientist and suggested that the conference room was set up and that they were ready for their meeting to begin. This was a miracle that Peter had been able to get Monica and Eva Rodriguez to delay their trip home and to agree to have this meeting with the university staff. So, Peter decided to limit the number of people involved to just Professor Nelson. Professor Nelson had insisted that Shelley, Peter's lab assistant be at the meeting to take notes and minutes of the meeting for a witness of the proceedings when Peter explained the importance and significance of the discussion. At first Peter did not think anything of the selection of Shelley at the meeting. Now, he was completely uncomfortable as he introduced the blond beauty to his Peruvian princess. He had no idea how awkward this was going to be. Peter had forgotten that he had told Monica everything about his relationship with Shelley during the three weeks that they had been kidnapped and held together. Peter was rather worried he had run into a hornet's nest when he saw Monica continue to gaze at Shelley long after the introductions were given. Shelley couldn't help but return the icy look, and the meeting room definitely seemed cooler than normal, like someone had suddenly turned up the air conditioning.

Peter was very cognizant of the importance and sensitive nature of the material they were about to witness. So, he again decided to lock the door and to make sure that everyone knew of the confidential nature of this meeting. He was adamant that secrecy was of the utmost importance. Peter expressed his desire that the notes be considered strictly top secret and only Professor Nelson and Eva Rodriguez would have copies of them. Next, he turned the lights off. Peter again went through the same photo presentation of the previous night, except this time he purposely omitted the last series of photos that included the sacred resting place of the Pizarros.

"Peter, this is fantastic....This is incredible...this is just simply wonderful! Why didn't you tell me that you had made a tunnel discovery?" The scientist was completely overwhelmed by the photo presentation. Professor Nelson's usual cautious and bland temperament was energized to a higher degree than Peter had ever known was possible for him.

"Professor Nelson, I have given my word to safeguard this discovery and the treasure. The golden treasure in the tunnel chamber is of course the property of the Peruvian government and her people. I have not told you of the significance of these two women before you. Monica and her mother own the restaurant above the tunnel entrance. Monica is the one that helped me find the treasure and they will not allow us to share it with the world unless we agree to certain conditions. They are part of the Incan leadership of Cusco, and are quite concerned about how this knowledge will be exposed to the world and to the Peruvian people and how we can safeguard the treasure. If it is not handled properly, they will not allow us to proceed. We need to give them some assurances that the university will work with the Peruvian government at the highest levels to control and protect the discovery. In return, the university and Balboa Explorations will get credit for the treasure discovery and will benefit financially for helping to promote it and develop a strategy that will be designed to encourage tourism to Cusco, Peru," Peter stated enthusiastically. "These are their terms!"

"Peter, I think that we can agree to these conditions of course. But, I would like to have a meeting with the Dean of the College and the President of the University. To get the ball rolling we will need their cooperation and financial support," Professor Nelson said thoughtfully. "If we can get in to see them today while your guests are here, it would be better. Actually, the sooner the better, then they can decide if they trust us."

"Professor, what Monica and her mother want are assurances that we will do this properly. They speak English well enough….Please tell them that you will promise as I do to protect the treasure and to help safeguard the secrets of the tunnels and make sure that these things are exploited in a manner that will best help the people of Peru. They do not want anyone else to see the pictures, but us, until the time comes to make a public news conference."

"Peter, I promise you all that I will do my best. Eva and Monica, I will be pleased to be involved with Peter in this project. I promise you that we will guard the treasure and help you to keep it safe for the Peruvian people. You have entrusted us in a great responsibility and a tremendous adventure. I hope we will be completely worthy of such a trust. Thank you Eva and Monica for coming here today with Peter, thank you." Professor Nelson was very sincere in his promise and it relieved Eva Rodriguez enough that she was now comfortable to continue to meet with the university president and faculty. Peter had known all along that if he could finally get Eva and Monica into a room with his graduate professor then they would know how great a man he was and they would allow Peter to proceed with his plan and be successful. Everyone in the room knew that eventually this find would be made public because of the GPR study and the intentions of Balboa Explorations. Peter's plan would just let the Peruvian people do it on their time table and to their best interest.

"Peter, I just don't know you anymore. You are obsessed with this treasure and this 'project' of yours. We have been cooped up in this motel for two days and drug through countless meetings. I am tired and I want to go home. My two week vacation is almost up anyway, and I've spent more time touring your campus than anything else," moaned Monica. They sat together in a food court at a nearby mall. "I have hardly seen you by myself for days, and this is the first chance that I have had to even talk to you, alone. While Mom is in the bathroom, I just wanted to ask you one simple question. Do you love me?"

There it was! It was the actual question that Peter was trying to avoid for months. It had finally caught up with him. There was definitely commitment attached to the affirmative answer and this is what Peter was trying to sidestep. Peter reached over the table and took Monica's hand and looked directly into her eyes. "Monica, be patient with me. This is a big step and a big commitment for me. I don't know if I am ready to answer that!" He looked up and with his free hand he waved it around the room. "I love this food court and my life has been very similar to this place which is my favorite place to eat. I love Quiznos, but I like to dine at Taco Bell, A& W, and the Japanese place for variety. My most favorite by far is Quiznos, but I'm worried that if I ate there everyday then it would get boring. I like exploring new things and keeping my options open. Someday there might be something else that will come along that I will like even more," mused Peter.

Monica just sat there and stared at him, incredulously. Slowly she pulled her hand away from him. Peter could see that the analogy had not gone down well. "Shelley is supposed to get married in two months to this creep and I'm just waiting to see what happens," Peter rushed on in swampy territory. "Her boyfriend, Jason, is three years older than her, and is a rich guy that is head of security at the Mirage hotel in Las Vegas. He buys her everything and spoils her rotten. I don't like him at all. I don't think that it is going to work out and she will eventually come to her senses. You know I met him a couple of weeks ago, and I seriously think that there is something wrong with the guy. I just can't put my finger on it, but there is something definitely wrong with him," continued Peter.

Monica's blank stare was starting to change gradually. Her face was turning redder by the minute and Peter was rattling on without a clue, and he was oblivious to the effect that this conversation was having on Monica. The chair made a terrible screeching sound on the tile floor as Monica pushed it back and stood in front of him. With a terrible angry voice and an expression that scared Peter out of his wits she said, "Do you *love* me?" Silence...the busy noisy cafeteria was quite, everyone in the whole food court was looking at their table. The embarrassed look on Peter's face, and no response, was enough to know the answer. Monica turned abruptly and started walking away. Peter was up and walking after her.

"Monica, we haven't finished eating. Where are you going?" Peter asked afraid that he had said something wrong.

"I am going to the restroom to find my mother." She turned to face him. "Your mother is picking us up this afternoon to take us back to the ranch. We will then get some transportation, the bus or something, to take us to the airport tomorrow and back to Peru where they don't have a Quiznos restaurant!" The angry retort had humiliated Peter, and he didn't know what to say. Peter followed after her like a wounded puppy dog.

"But, Monica, I do like you very much. You have become more than just my best friend. I thought we could talk about anything. I do care for you very much," explained Peter. It was too little too late, and Monica entered the bathroom door without even looking back.

The light blue seats at the airport had originally felt very soft and comfortable. Now, two hours later they were hard as rock and Eva and Monica were still waiting. Their flight was delayed to get the necessary maintenance clearance, and these same chairs had become very hard and uncomfortable. "Mother, can you believe that Peter compared me to his favorite restaurant, Quiznos? I was astonished…no appalled….no that is not it ….I was humiliated. He wanted to try all the restaurants and even explore new ones before he picked the one he was going to eat at the rest of his life. How stupid is that? In fact, come to think of it… I'm not sure if I am even his favorite, Quiznos!" A sudden realization crossed her mind and made her even madder. "Mom, I'm not sure if I am Quiznos or if that other girl, Shelley, is Quiznos and I am just an A&W! How stupid is that?"

"Monica calm down. It is all over. We are going home. You can pick out a nice Peruvian boy and we can go back to our previous lives. It will be all good. I assure you, there will be other guys to pick from. In fact I have a few in mind already that I would be happy to suggest," joked Eva Rodriguez.

"Mom, I just love him. He is so exasperating. But, I just love him. In two more months he will be a doctor of geology, but he is so, so stupid!"

"Don't worry about him anymore, Monica. You're going to get yourself all worked up, again. This is not good. Forget about it, and let's talk about something else," soothed Eva.

"Mom, I left the dress at the ranch on my bed!" confessed Monica. "I also left a note for Isabela to find. I told her that I hoped that she could get her money back from the dress shop. And that someday I hoped that she could buy me something as her daughter-in-law!" said Monica sadly.

"Well, that should stir some things up in the Martin household," laughed Eva. With the amount of apologies and concern that Don Jose had expressed while he was driving us to the airport and you leaving the dress for Isabela, Peter won't be able to go home for a month," Eva laughed heartily. "I would give anything to be there and to listen in on some of those conversations around the Martin Hacienda in the next few days." Eva looked at her daughter with the big sad eyes. "Come on we need to cheer you up!"

"Oh, mother, I've put you into such a terrible position. Now, the tunnel and the treasure is exposed and our lives with be changed forever. Peter said that it is by far the largest treasure ever found anywhere in the world in the modern era, and it is worth millions. The Peruvian government if they advertise and market the discovery properly will be able to make billions out of the increased tourism. Peter says that there is enough treasure that they could even lease out several displays to museums around the world. It would even further promote the main display in the tunnel in Cusco and would bring incredible wealth to the people of Peru. Hopefully, we can use that wealth to stabilize our economy and bring better living conditions to our people. He is so smart, he has it all planned out. We will buy the building next to the Main Cathedral and turn it into a small museum and office building. The building would also house air filtration and air ventilation equipment that would be necessary to make the tunnel continually safe for tours. The people would exit the tour through the basement passage of our restaurant and they could even eat at our restaurant if they are hungry. Peter says that he will build walls around the Pizarro tomb and not allow anyone access to it, seal it up forever. Peter is so smart, he has an answer and a plan for everything."

Eva just looked at her daughter in amazement. Oh, how she loved her. Then a serious thought came across her mind. Monica saw the change of expression in her countenance. "What! What's the matter Mom?"

"Oh, I was just thinking that I am going to have to be on top of my game to be able to sell Peter's plan to the Incan Elders and to my brother." Eva said thoughtfully. "It may not be as easy to convince them as it was to convince you!"

Chapter Notes – Chapter 23
No notes.

Picture of the modern downtown areas of Lima

Chapter 24

Lima International Airport – Present Day

It was a grey cloudy day in Lima which was unusual. It even looked like it was going to rain and it can go for years without raining in Lima. The city of Lima typically has hot sunny, muggy days year round. The sun's rays are filtered through various layers of polluted atmosphere depending on how much breeze there is associated with the particular day. With nearly nine million people living, breathing, and driving cars, the modern metropolitan city has become dependant on the cleansing action of the Pacific Ocean's Humboldt winds. Monica and Eva Rodriguez stood in the lines of people surrounding the baggage carousel waiting for it to start up. "Well, we are finally back home in Peru, Mother. What do you want to do tonight here in Lima before we leave for Cusco in the morning?" asked Monica.

"Oh, I don't know, surprise me. This is your city with all of your college friends. You can decide. I'm actually very tired and I would be happy for just a warm soft bed." Their conversation broke off with the sound of the carousel conveyor motor starting. It was the signal that their bags would be streaming onto the long conveyor any moment.

"Well, as soon as we have our bags and we are out of the terminal, then I will call Emma and see if she has room for us tonight. Then, we can go out to get something to eat. I have my favorite little Argentine restaurant a little ways away from her apartment that I would like you to try," continued Monica. A bag with a brightly colored green ribbon came into view. Monica moved quickly to pick up the first of their four suitcases. It wasn't long until they had all four bags and their carryon baggage all neatly stacked on a porter's trolley. The porter gave the baggage claim tickets to the security officer and for the first time in two weeks Monica and Eva stepped out into the warm sea breeze of the Peruvian coast that seemed so familiar to them.

The scene outside the terminal was pandemonium as always. There were several men descending on them already trying to hustle a cab fare or give them a tour of the city. Monica and Eva ignored them all. To actually acknowledge and speak to one would have sealed a deal or encouraged them even further, so a simple 'no' was all that was required. "Emma, my roommate, will be at work, Mother, so I'll just leave a message at her apartment with my cell phone," Monica said while she was fumbling around in her purse for the electronic gadget. "Then we can get a cab."

"Don't worry! Look who is here to meet us!" shouted Eva over the melee all about them. Ten yards away and walking towards them was Carlos Rodriguez, Eva's brother. He was the tallest man, at six foot two inches, that anyone could remember in the Rodriguez family. In his early thirties, tall and handsome, Carlos Rodriguez stuck out of the crowd, and Eva had always been so proud of her young brother. Carlos wore a nice light blue business suit and was holding a large white sign with the word 'Rodriguez' printed in bold black letters. He was smiling and yelling wildly for them as he spotted his two relatives coming out of the terminal building.

"Eva….Eva, I have a van waiting for us!" Carlos yelled over all the noise and commotion. "Let's get out of here." He motioned for the porter to follow them with the baggage. Uncle Carlos kissed them both on the cheek and then quickly guided them to his waiting new small white Mercedes van parked in the loading zone with a waiting driver. Eva gave the porter a five Soles coin after he had loaded the four large suitcases into the rear of the brand new van. The porter wanted more. After a brief conversation with the man about trying to overcharge travelers for a job he was already getting paid for and that tipping was still voluntary in the country of Peru, he went silent. The man did not take too kindly to the rebuke or lecture, but just hastily put the coin in his pocket and was off to find another passenger in need of his services. "Eva …Eva, ….usually that porter would receive twice that amount for carrying your bags," chuckled Carlos. "You have to get with the times!" Carlos laughed again.

"I don't care…I think it is an outrage what they charge, and their aggressive behavior is deplorable. They are all just like vultures waiting to eat you as soon as you come out into the light of day. I'm truly disgusted with it all!" Eva retorted acting very offended.

Monica giggled at this exchange between brother and sister, and then all at once a realization came over her. "I am certainly my mother's daughter. Now, I know where this sense of righteous values comes from," Monica thought to herself. It was an experience that was actually quite revealing to spend so much time with her mother. Monica was enjoying every minute of their adventure together. "How come you are here to pick us up, and how did you know when we were coming home?" asked Monica after the van had started out of the airport terminal and onto the main highway into Lima center.

"Oh, I am here in Lima today on business and our office has you scheduled to be back to work tomorrow. So, I just figured that you would be flying in today, and I decided to come here to pick up my favorite niece and only sister," Carlos said with a smile. "Besides, since you work for me, I need to know what's happening all the time, don't I?" he chuckled, again. "Boy, the Department of Tourism here in Lima has a lot better vehicles than we do in Cusco. What do you think of this new van? We're really riding in style, today."

"Yes, it is very nice. Uncle, could you please have the driver take us to 2512 Portico Street. It is only three blocks from the university. Thanks... Uncle Carlos," Monica directed. Carlos Rodriguez repeated the address to the driver with a grin. A half an hour later and the bus was taking a more southern route than Monica had expected. "Uncle Carlos this isn't the way to my friend's apartment. Where are we going?"

"I hope it is okay if we make one stop first. I have an errand to do for the department. Then, we will take you over to the university," Carlos responded casually. The conversation continued about the things that were going on in Cusco since they had left. Carlos had to give a little dialogue about each one of his kids and how they were doing in school. He brought Monica up to speed on the office news and how everyone was excited to get her back home to Cusco. Carlos had even been to the restaurant a few times to look in on the staff and to see how they were doing. The assistant manager had not had any major problems, but it was the first time she had actually run the store by herself for any length of time. Carlos had helped answer a few questions, but he didn't know much about the business. Soon, the van pulled up to a nice-looking two storey house that actually looked more like a warehouse than someone's house. "Come on in, I have something to show you. I think you'll find this very interesting!" Carlos said with an excited tone to his voice. Eva and Monica were curious. They did not know that Carlos knew much about Lima or spent any time here except on business meetings for the department. So, this was going to be fun, more like a scavenger hunt or an exploration than a party or the ballet, but hey, you take fun wherever you can find it. After traveling for two days, Monica and Eva were excited to be out doing something anyway, instead of sitting in the van.

Inside the gated front courtyard the walkway went directly into the building with only one front door. Monica had not even noticed what street they were on or the address. She just followed her mother, dutifully. As the group entered through the door, a musty smell permeated the air. The main rooms were loaded with all sorts of relics that didn't look much like antiques, just junk. It was a warehouse of old materials used in tourism conferences and media campaigns. Monica recognized some of the backdrops and props that had been in television commercials and other media events. Without a word, Carlos led them down a corridor and finally down two flights of stairs. They entered a basement room that looked more like an apartment than part of the warehouse. "Well, here we are," Carlos laughed as he extended his arms to show them the full extent of the room. "This will be your home for a while, so enjoy it and get comfortable! Make yourselves at home. I'll be back in a few hours!"

"What are you talking about, Carlos!" stammered Eva with an astonished look. "We're not staying here. We're going to stay with Monica's friend, tonight!" Carlos just stared at her and then he started to laugh again. The driver that was standing behind Monica ripped her purse off her shoulder. In one quick move he extracted the cell phone from out of the contents and handed it to Carlos.

"Hey, Uncle, you can't have my cell phone. I need it to call…" Monica never got to finish her sentence.

"I'll just hold on to this for safe keeping." Carlos said with a sneer. It was a look that Eva had never seen before and it was unsettling.

"Carlos, what is going on here? I demand to know right now." Eva Rodriguez was not annoyed anymore, but mad.

"Oh, don't worry big sister….I will take care of you!" Carlos and the driver started walking backward to the door, and with an evil laugh they were gone. The metal door locked with an audible click and then there was a rasping, scraping sound of a dead bolt sliding into its latch. Monica could hear footsteps and muffled talking fading away until there was no sound at all.

"Mother, what is happening? What is going on? Is Uncle Carlos crazy; is this a gag or a game that he is playing with us?" Monica was frightened now and with the look from her mother she could tell that her mother felt the same way.

"I don't know Monica. I don't think so. There has to be some explanation. Don't panic, when Carlos comes back we will get to the bottom of this." Eva was suddenly very tired and looked around the rather large bare room. There were two single beds at the back of the room and Eva just flopped down on the first one that she came to. "Well, it isn't a three star hotel, but at least it has a bed." Eva was exhausted.

"Mother, we are being held here as prisoners and against our will and all you can think about it sleep?" screamed Monica. She ran to the big metal door and turned the door knob…Nothing. Monica then looked around the room. She started to run from one wall to the next, touching each wall and corner as she went. Finally, at the back of the room near the beds she came to the only other door. It opened into a small bathroom with a toilet, sink, and a makeshift shower unit. That was it. The room had no windows at all! And it only had one outside door that was bolted. On the dingy light-blue plastered walls hung only one travel poster of the City of Lima, nothing else. The large room was devoid of any furniture except for a small wooden table with two chairs and the two beds. Two wires hung down from the ceiling with light bulbs attached to them which provided their light. Monica circled the room twice feeling trapped like a rat in a cage checking out the perimeter of the enclosure. Finally, just like her mother she flopped on the other bed, exhausted.

An hour later footsteps and the sound of the latch opening, woke Monica with a start. One of Carlos's henchmen, a well dressed pock-faced fellow appeared in the doorway with another hard case little man with a large automatic weapon strapped to his side. "We have been through your suitcases and are returning them to you, minus a few little things. We didn't want you to hurt yourselves or have something sharp to dig yourselves a tunnel with," he said with an evil laugh.

Monica didn't wait for them to place the bags inside the door. She just rushed through the little man and got half way through the opening where she was met by two other large guys all dressed in the same blue security uniform. "Whoa there, wait….where do you think you're going little girl? You can't leave us so soon. Carlos says that you need to stay and get real comfortable." The pock-faced man said with a snide derisive expression. One security man lifted her off the ground and quite literally carried her back through the door and threw Monica on the ground. The door was locked and bolted again. Eva bounded off her bed and was at Monica's side quickly. Monica was crying, but uninjured.

"Mother, what is going on? Why are they doing this?" she managed to say in-between sobs. "What is going to happen to us?"

"I don't know.…I just don't know. But, I intend on strangling my little brother when he comes back. I'll find out what he is up to, believe me. I'll wring it out of his handsome neck, and pull his tie up so tight it strangles him," Eva said with a caustic angry voice.

A few hours later Carlos and his men had returned as promised. They were not kind or patient, but got right to the point. Both Monica and Eva were seated at the table and other chairs were brought in, and they settled into a lengthy interrogation about their trip to the United States. "I'll ask you just one more time. Why is the University of California calling my boss, the Director of Tourism for Peru? Why do they want to set up some high level meetings with the President of our country? What have you been up to in the United States?" coaxed Carlos again in an exasperated tone. "If you do not tell me what I want to know, then I will have my friends rough you up, and I will take pleasure in watching them do it." This little interrogation was going into the third hour with no results on either side.

"Okay, Carlos, I'll compromise with you. You tell me why you are doing this thing, and I will tell you why we went to California, Okay?" Eva said. She was very angry and for the first time seeing a side to her brother that she did not know existed.

"Very well, I'll tell you that being the only male member left in our family; it should fall to me to rule Peru. I am the rightful heir to the Inca throne. Several of the Elders agree with me. I have led the crusade against the government for several years now. The rebels revere me and will follow me to the death. Not only do I control the 'Shinning Path', but several other organizations. I am a leader of a secret society that upholds the sacred ways of the Inca." The speech flowed from Carlos like he had been practicing it for days. Eva's eyes were fixated on Carlos and she was utterly astonished at his narration.

"What!" cried Monica. "You had me kidnapped? Why?...."

"Sure...why not? I had to show my associates that I would sacrifice my own niece for the good of our secret organization! But, I never wanted them to kill you. That was Hugo's idea and I had to eliminate him because he was out of control. We just needed the money," Carlos said nonchalantly.

"You are pure evil, little brother. So, it's all about money?" seethed Eva.

"No, it's all about being the Inca King, and the money!" said Carlos disdainfully.

"That's llama dung!! You can't be King! And you know it. The Incan Elders have anointed me the Queen and ruler of the Incas right after my husband died. They have placed the Royal Fringe upon my head and placed the Inca bat-hair cape about my shoulders signifying that I have been chosen to rule the Incas." Eva broadcasted triumphantly to all those in the room and loud enough for everyone to know and to make sure that the guards did not mistake who they had taken prisoner.

"What?..." It was all Monica could say as she looked at her mother completely astonished. She was seeing her own mother in a light that she had never before known. "What are you saying mother? You are a Queen?...Queen of the Incas?"

"Yes, my daughter...our blood line is the most pure. The right has been given to us. Of course we are not recognized by the government or by the Catholic Church. But, hopefully, someday, then the right to govern our people will be returned to us again." Monica couldn't say a thing. She was just totally shocked and bewildered. Monica got up off from her chair and walked over to her bed and just sat down on it staring at her mother with a blank face.

"I'm sorry, my sister, but your time is over and now it falls to me. I am the new leader of the Inca. You will abdicate your crown or you will never go free. If you do not answer my questions, then my men will have to kill Monica. Then, if I am not satisfied with what I want to know, then I will have you killed as well. Now, tell me why did you go to the United States? Tell me if that young American, Peter, is involved. Come on Eva, I told you why we are having this little conversation, now it is your turn!" Carlos was being more patient and trying to calm his sister down. He was guessing, now, and she knew it.

Eva was appalled at the indifference that he valued their lives. "Why… you are a little scorpion. You are the most evil man I have ever known. You are not fit to rule our people at all." Eva screamed. "I don't think we'll tell you anything. Carlos motioned to his men to leave. Carlos turned to the door as well.

"You will, Eva…you will." Carlos countered. The door slammed shut and the dead bolt was scraped into place.

Exactly five hours from their last visit came a knock at the door, again, according to Monica's watch. "Are you decent, are you dressed?" It was Carlos's familiar voice. I am here for another little chat. According to Monica's watch it was just after midnight.

"Do we have to do this again, Carlos? Monica and I are very tired from traveling. "How about let's talk again in the morning?" Eva beseeched her brother.

"No, I'd rather have this discussion tonight." Carlos unbolted the metal door and threw it back wide for several of his men to enter the room with him. Tonight the suit coat was missing as well as his tie. It looked like Carlos meant business. Two of the security guards grabbed Monica and Eva and bodily threw them into the chairs at the table. This time the guards tied their hands behind the back of their chair with plastic ties. "Okay, the way this game works is I will ask you a question. If you answer it correctly then we can move on to the next question. If you answer the question incorrectly then Gustavo here will strike you across the face. Now if we have your attention then we can begin at the beginning. Why did you go to California?" asked Carlos politely.

"I've said all I going to say to you Carlos. I don't want to talk to you anymore. Carlos just nodded to Gustavo and with one slap Eva screamed as her head snapped back. Her lip was bleeding and a big red welt in the shape of a hand was now imprinted on her face.

"No, Uncle, don't touch her again…I'll tell you," screamed Monica.

"Well, that's more like it," soothed Carlos with a nasty grin, he was starting to enjoy this.

"We went to America to see Peter. I wanted to find out if Peter loved me and what his intentions were. Mother wanted to come along to chaperone me. We stayed at his parent's house for a few days. Peter's mother bought me a fabulous dress that I wore to a party that they had in my honor. Peter showed us around the university. But, he couldn't decide if I was a Quiznos restaurant or an A& W. So, I got mad at him and we left and came home to Peru…" Monica offered to continue the monologue, but Carlos cut her off.

"You love this young man, Monica?" questioned Carlos flabbergasted. "You've only known him a couple of months, and he is not Peruvian. Did your mother tell you that you can not marry someone who is not Peruvian?" Carlos said incredulously.

"I did not know that Mom was the Incan Queen, or that you were such a scoundrel!" replied Monica in a huff. "Why does everyone want to tell me how to live my life? And, who I should marry? It isn't fair."

"Why does the University of California want to have all of these meetings? What is going on?" Carlos continued on to the next of his questions, trying to focus on the matter at hand.

"Oh that is simple." Monica started to explain things again to her Uncle Carlos. She glanced at her mother who was keeping silent, but raised an eyebrow as if to signal Monica to keep quite. "Mom promised Peter that she would talk to the priests and the Incan Elders about getting permission to excavate a tunnel opening that we found in the fortress of Sacsahuaman if he would return to Peru and marry me!" lied Monica with a straight face. Carlos couldn't believe his ears.

"What?....She can't do that. She has already promised the government, the Church hierarchy, me, and everyone else that we would adamantly oppose any excavation in the city of Cusco. We are all in agreement so, that we can safeguard sacred our city and our Inca heritage. "There is something more. I can feel it; you are not telling me the truth." He nodded again to Gustavo who took a swing at Monica this time, almost knocking her and the chair over at the same time. Monica righted the chair just in time, but was crying with pain.

"Carlos, no, you can't do this..." yelled Eva. "Sacsahuaman is technically out of the city limits of Cusco, you know that! You mean buzzard!" Carlos seemed puzzled momentarily. Something did not seem right here somehow, but he couldn't put his finger on it quite yet. He needed time to think to study it out in his mind.

"I am returning to Cusco, tomorrow," seethed Carlos. "I will tell everyone that you have been detained in California by this young man who wants to marry you. I will investigate this matter on my own and see if you are telling me the truth. In time you will tell me everything. In the mean time, Eva, my men are instructed to give you all the pen and paper that you need. I want you to write down for me everything that you can remember from the Sacred Quipu. It will be mine from now on. I will go to your apartment and find it. You will tell me everything that I want to know."

"Carlos, you know that I can't do that. It is against our sacred Inca law. 'The Rememberer' has to memorize the Sacred Quipu according to the knots. It is unlawful to write it down. The Incan Elders will kill me, if I do not guard it with my life. It is punishable by death to do such a thing!" exclaimed Eva. She had always known that Carlos was jealous of her, because she was 'The Rememberer'. He had never been granted that privilege, but he had always wanted it. And now he did not deserve it.

"You chose, dear sister, either they can kill you, or I will kill you if you don't write it down!"

"We are hungry....Can we have something to eat?" begged Eva.

"My men are instructed to visit you each day. If you have written things down for me, they are going to feed you. If nothing is written you will go hungry! Tomorrow they will feed you if you have written at least a page. Do you understand?" demanded Carlos.

Eva just nodded.

"I will need the Sacred Quipu if I am to write a full account of its meaning and what the knots stand for. I cannot do it without the Quipu here in my hands. Maybe you should let us return to Cusco and I can read it for you there," whispered Eva.

"No…I will bring it to you!" Carlos turned and strode out through the door without even saying good bye. One by one his cohorts followed him out the big metal door. The door was slammed shut again. The bolt slid into place with the familiar scraping sound, and they were gone.

Chapter Notes – Chapter 24

The knotted string quipu was used as an accounting system in the Incan culture. It was continued to be used by the natives even after the conquest. The size of the knots and the colors used made it possible to record quantities with extreme precision. Historical quipu were used to record outstanding episodes and events of the Inca dynasties. There are many quipu mantles that are on display at the various museums in Peru.

Picture of the modern Presidential Palace which was originally the governors mansion built by Francisco Pizarro

Chapter 25

Lima, Peru – Modern Day

Monica had laid on her bed so long today that her back was sore. The walls of the room were an antiseptic light-blue plaster and the floors made of polished ceramic tiles. In the morning and evening the room was extremely cold with no rugs or carpet to cover the floor. Monica wished that she had warmer blankets since the building had no central heating. It had been five days to the best of her knowledge since their detainment in Lima. Monica had made a ritual of walking around the room several times each day and doing as many calisthenics and exercises as she could remember how to do. To keep busy she would go through this routine every morning and evening. But, she soon had lost track of the days and nights and which day of the week it was. Even though she had a watch, she was losing all track of time. The most important event of the day was taking a shower. If she let the water heat up in the small electric heater above the shower head then she could even have warm water for at least forty-five seconds. If they needed anything cleaned then they had to wash the items out by hand in the bathroom sink. Even their sheets, they had decided to wash by hand because they weren't certain who had used them before. It wasn't like they didn't have any time for all these activities.

Eva would not let Monica talk freely in their room because she suspected that Jose had bugged the room before they arrived. However, they had had several interesting discussions in the small bathroom with the water running to drown out any sound that might get picked up electronically. Eva had written just enough down each day to appease her captors and receive their daily rations. Actually, the food wasn't that bad. Monica suspected that the guards were using a restaurant nearby. They would only bring them two meals a day, but the quantities were more than sustaining. It didn't appear that there was more than one guard on duty anymore, because they had the same one for the last four days. Now, today was the first day for the new guy's shift. Monica wanted to start up a discussion and make friends with him. She thought that maybe she could bribe him to deliver a letter for her that she had written to Peter. Monica had written the letter in English and a bit vague with a coded message that she was certain that Peter would figure out. The guard took the letter, examined it, and when he saw that it was written in English, he promptly ripped it into shreds.

Now, Monica and her mother sat in silence. Since, the guard would not return for another six hours, there was really nothing to do at all. Monica was bored. She went back to her bed, and laid down. The room seemed cold to her, so she pulled her covers over her. She gazed at the ceiling and then the wall. Monica couldn't sleep, she wasn't tired. On the wall was the tourism poster. For the first time Monica noticed that it was a picture of the Presidential Government Building here in Lima. The building had started out to be the palatial home for Governor Francisco Pizarro. Of course in the time of Pizarro the palace was quite humble compared to the fabulous building that stands on the same grounds today. Francisco had returned to the sea coast from Cusco with his young bride, Lacoya Ines. At an old age, the mountain air and altitude did not agree with Francisco very much and he wanted to be close to the coast where he could look out on the sea once again. Of course, officially, he would establish his seat of government here in Lima because of its beautiful seaport potential and so that his communication with the outside world could be more efficient especially with Panama and Spain.

Francisco now had at his command a huge supply of wealth and an unlimited supply of labor. The Peruvian slaves were not free labor. He had to feed and clothe these people, every day. Pizarro in the wisdom of his old age had really figured out that if he treated the people well, then he would be able to accomplish much with the encouragement of the taskmasters whip and plenty to eat. Francisco, however, did not want to be such a fierce tyrant that the native work force would rebel against his rule and create anarchy. So, it was a fine balance that he needed to exercise. With the help of the Inca's daughter and their queen, Francisco knew he could realistically create the ideal kingdom. His goal was to teach his people a better, more civilized way of life. He truly wanted to teach them Christianity and baptize the whole country into the Holy Catholic Church. His own wife was now baptized, spoke and read Spanish fluently, and was even learning Latin so that she could more fully understand the weekly Mass ceremony performed by her beloved priests.

The Catholic priests had taken a particular interest in Lacoya Ines because of her intelligence and beauty. Her willingness to learn the new European ways and embrace the new empire was very endearing to everyone, not only the priests. Francisco, the governor himself, could never be bothered to learn to read and write, but would rather dictate his letters or orders to others. He did not want to waste time learning these difficult things at this late stage in his life. Francisco would rather practice his skills as a swordsman or marksman with a blunderbuss than to waste away his time reading what someone else had written. Pizarro had his priorities elsewhere. He was the acclaimed champion swordsman amongst his men as long as he could remember. He had never lost in a mock battle or even in practice. It was legendary throughout all of Peru and the New World actually, even as an old man in his seventy-first year of age, that he had never been beaten. Francisco was the champion swordsman of the entire Peruvian Empire. Mostly though, Francisco spent his time planning and supervising the construction of his new capital City. Now, Francisco was transforming it into his city and his kingdom. Francisco loved his new world and new kingdom. He had fought hard for it. Francisco was determined to rebuild Lima just the way that he wanted it. He had come to Peru as a conqueror, and now he was a builder of a new nation, and a new city.

July 26th 1541

The day had dawned with a clear blue sky and the sun peaking over the lush green foothills of the Andean Mountains to the East. Today was Sunday, an important day because Francisco Pizarro had some prestigious guests coming for supper from Panama. Francisco had risen early and dressed in his finest Spanish suit of tailored clothes. His intention was to give a lengthy tour of the city to his guests. This fine house that he had built was really a palace, befitting a king. It would serve as his governor's mansion, but it was his design and he was quite proud of the structure. It surely would have made even some of his colleagues in Spain envious. It had taken 2000 Peruvian artisans and 300 Spanish overseers more than two years to complete. And the finishing touches were still in progress.

Next, across the central square of the city, was the new Cathedral of Lima which was only partially completed, but it already had at least one chapel that was functional. A second Cathedral for the Franciscans had already been started into construction as well. On the other side of the square would be his government buildings which would house the offices of the Crown. The clerks and officials of Spain seemed to be more numerous these days than Francisco's military officers. Pizarro was very pleased with all of the progress in a very short period of time that they had made to turn this ancient city into a thriving, bustling, seaport city. It was truly a 'City of Kings'.

Francisco had remembered when they first arrived, Lacoya Ines would not allow him to build or desecrate the nearby religious citadel called Pachacamac. Lima, the City of Kings, as it was called anciently was already a large city mostly laid to ruins by civil war, the devastation of small pox, and the Spanish Conquest. There were inside the city much building material already. The Spanish used the ancient Inca foundations and knocked down many Inca palaces, temples, and important buildings to rebuild a new city on top of the old. A similar approach had been used to rebuild the city of Cusco. It was part of the Spanish concept of conquering the heathen Indian population. To begin a 'New World' and build it properly would require a smothering of the old culture and a complete destruction of the old religion. They would need to completely change the Peruvian culture into a new entity designed and formatted after their own Spanish empire.

Francisco Pizarro had succeeded where most men would have failed. The sheer breadth of the task was so enormous that most people did not realize how hard it had been to accomplish. Francisco truly believed that God had inspired him. God had driven him on to greatness, that he might be an instrument in His hands to do a mighty work. Francisco had tamed this new frontier, this new land. Francisco had a clear understanding that his work had been directed by a higher power. He had felt it from the beginning of his quest, and now in the twilight of his life and career, he had much to be thankful for. God had truly blessed him with the finest house in the 'New World', the most beautiful, loving wife, and wealth beyond his wildest dreams. What more could a man ask for? How could he deny that God had truly blessed him? To be young again or to have more children were all beyond the reach of his mortal dreams. This morning Francisco wanted to pause at the cathedral and give thanks to his God in Heaven for all of these important blessings. He also felt a need for his priest to give him absolution for any sins that he might have committed along the way of his conquest of Peru. Surely, God would forgive him some of his trespasses in comparison to the great accomplishments that he had done in the name of God and to establish His Holy Kingdom here in Peru.

The guests would start arriving soon. Francisco also wanted his priest to take him down into the ancient Inca catacombs under the cathedral where Pizarro had hidden and sealed up his treasure for safekeeping. King Charles V had required of him in his financial contract a fifth part of all of the treasure that was accumulated into the common treasury. Francisco had also required of the same dispersal a two fifth's part to run the government and supply his army. Of the two main dispersals (Cajamarca and Cusco) Francisco had received more than 3000 Kg of gold and 7000 Kg of silver. There had been several smaller dispersals as well that had also netted Francisco even more wealth. What the Spanish officers and clerks did not know was that Francisco and his brothers had bartered and traded for much more of the Inca wealth using horses, weapons, and supplies from the general arsenal to obtain much of the remaining gold and treasure. The brothers had set up two caches, one in Cusco and the other here in Lima. These caches had been secreted away from the knowledge of anyone except for the Pizarros themselves and a few trusted individuals.

In reality the cost of doing the government business was actually quite low compared to the work that was being accomplished in this time of peace. Francisco could put his men of the army to work on all of the building projects to keep them occupied, but still have them under arms the moment that peaceful circumstances changed. The taxes levied against the people were not particularly burdensome, but returned enough to actually maintain the army and provide for the needs of the government. Food was plentiful, easy to grow, and cheap. In reality, Francisco could still add to his treasure room periodically with the excess proceeds that would flow in to him.

The priest opened the heavy wooden door that only he had the key to. It was specifically hung around his neck for this one purpose. Pizarro had made a duplicate key only yesterday for himself. He had not told the priest, his brothers or anyone as yet except his wife that he had already made arrangements to transfer the treasure permanently to a specially designed chamber underneath the Temple of The Women in Pachacamac. For the help that the priesthood were giving Pizarro in guarding the treasure, Francisco had contracted to give the Church 10% of the treasure to adorn their cathedrals when the construction was finished. His priest had assured him that such an action of graciousness would ensure that after death he would surely be canonized by the Pope in Rome, and achieve Sainthood. The other cache in Cusco would also be guarded by the Catholic priests and in return a similar ten percent of the treasure would be able to be utilized in the adornment of the various chapels and cathedrals of Cusco.

It was a brilliant plan because Francisco did not then need to employ his own men and valuable troops to guard the cache, and it could be kept secret easier as well. Some of his men he did not trust anyway with his accumulated fortune. The continued cathedral construction and use of the catacombs for rehabilitation of the natives required that he find a new place for his treasure cache here in Lima. Lacoya Ines as heir to the Inca throne and the actual owner of Pachacamac suggested the Temple of the Women. The location of the temple was one that the Spanish had already looted and explored. Every inch of the sacred citadel had been searched and now they were convinced that there could be nothing more found there. So, it would be a perfect hiding place for the future. The priests would build a small shrine or chapel next to the temple where they could monitor the treasure cache.

The plan was perfect and Francisco was very proud of himself. The priest opened the door and with a deep creak the door's rusty hinges swung open. Francisco lit his torch from the one hanging on the outside wall and entered the dark room. He lit five torches on one side while the priest lit five torches on the other side of the room. If only Atahualpa, the Inca prince, could see him, now. This treasure room held many times the amount of the original ransom for his life. Francisco inspected the long rows and stacks of gold and silver bullion bars that had been melted down for convenience of storage. There were also many rows of gold vases, animals, and trinkets of every size. Francisco had accumulated barrels of precious stones, such as emeralds, turquoise, amber, agate, and sapphires. The nicest artistic treasure pieces had been saved from the refiner's fire. Lacoya Ines was also pleased with the actions of her husband that had limited the amount of treasure that left the country and proud that her husband had developed this cache that would be deposited back into the sacred temple where it belonged.

His second cousin, Hernando Cortez, would have been most impressed and of course envious because this treasure room was many times the amount of gold and silver that he had ever extracted from his beloved Mexico. The worst concept would be for the King of Spain to actually know that Pizarro had accumulated this much wealth. It would be more than the King had ever dreamed of obtaining in all of his military conquests throughout Europe. The King himself would have come to Peru with his armies and his armadas to do battle with him had he known how wealthy Francisco had become. In deed, Francisco knew that he had become the wealthiest man in the known world, but he could not share that information with anyone. Any means possible would have been made to take it away from him. The world would covet and fight to obtain it, so it was better that Francisco just hide the treasure and not show it to the world. "What a waste!" Francisco said to the priest, "If only men were righteous and would look upon such wealth to do good instead of to kill and plunder! I leave it in your hands."

It was past time for breakfast, and Francisco was extremely hungry this morning. He did not feel like he was seventy-one. Many people said that he looked like the legendary Don Quixote, tall and skinny. Francisco was a dreamer, but he still had one hand touching reality. It was no doubt Lacoya Ines that made him feel so young. He was more than thirty years older than the Inca Princess, but she made him feel like a young man everyday. He could not believe his good fortune, because she actually loved him in return. Francisco had asked a special prayer for her in the Chapel this morning. Now, it was time for him to see what marvelous food she and her servants had prepared for him.

The evening supper, was the most elegant that had ever been served in the new dining hall of the governor's palace. The guests were satisfied and engaged in jovial conversation awaiting the dessert that was being prepared in the kitchen. The table was adorned with fine linen cloth made from the exquisitely fine wool of the Vicuna. An animal whose fur had been the most prized of all the herds of Peru. Lacoya Ines was a very capable hostess and she delighted in making her guests feel at home in their new mansion. They were always most impressed with the incredible gold dinnerware which was previously the service and place settings of the Inca King himself. Now, Lacoya Ines had access to all of the finest things of her country in conjunction with whatever Francisco could import from Spain. This combination provided a very impressive dinner ware setting, as well as helped acquire their elegant household furnishings for the mansion. Francisco had delighted in showing his guests around the city square and his own palace earlier before supper. These three dignitaries from Panama City were so impressed with the quality of the state that Pizarro had established in Peru that Francisco knew that they would give a very good report to their superiors in Panama and then eventually to the monarchy in Spain as well. Francisco had his color guard and the palace troop all in place for inspection earlier that day. As soon as the tour for the guests was over and supper had commenced, Pizarro had told the captain of the guard to dismiss their troop, and give the men the rest of the evening off, including the palace guard.

Francisco stood and held up his glass of fine Peruvian wine. "My dear Castilian brethren, may we make a toast...to His Majesty King Charles V!" Francisco said in a very stoic and reverent manner.

The governor's guests all stood at once and repeated, "To the King!"

"You may be seated. Gentleman of the High Court, I have one last request this night. Please join me in a toast to my queen! Princess Lacoya Ines Pizarro! She is your hostess and provider of this wonderful meal tonight!" With one accord the three guests joined the others surrounding the table to stand again in unison and toast together, "The Princess Lacoya Ines!"

There was a clamor in the hallway joining the dinning room. Several shrill shrieks and screams alerted the dinner party to an eminent emergency and danger.

Chapter Notes – Chapter 25

Francisco Pizarro returned to the coast in 1536 from the Andean Mountains and the capital city of Cusco. On the foundations of an ancient Incan city, Francisco built a new city, Lima, and made it his capital and the new capital of Peru. Lima was anciently the 'City of Kings' and it is still called that today as well, even though no king has ever lived in this city in modern memory. Francisco built a beautiful mansion for himself and started the construction of several Cathedrals in Lima. Francisco Pizarro is remembered not only for being the conqueror of Peru and first Governor, but also for being the founder of one of the largest cities in the world, Lima, Peru.

Main Cathedral in Lima, Peru built in the 16th Century

Chapter 26

Lima, Peru – July 26, 1541

The clamor from the hallway continued and grew until the screams abruptly ceased almost as quickly as they began. Four heavily armed conquistadors burst through the doorway. They were fully dressed in battle armor and wielded bucklers, shields, and swords. The upside down cross on the shield was a symbol of the 'Men of Chile' a renegade remnant of the army of the late Diego de Almagro. Two of Pizarro's servants quickly stepped in front of the intruders and were at once brutally dispatched by single blows of their sharp Spanish swords. Francisco and two of the guests that also had their dress ceremonial swords drew them as they prepared to receive the enemy. At the ripe old age of seventy-one years of age, Pizarro still practiced daily his swordsmanship exercises. The first conquistador was across the dinner table and attacked Francisco with a quick thrust of his sword, which Francisco side stepped easily. Then Pizarro ran him through before he had a chance to counter the surprising quickness of the governor. Another four of the enemy came through the dinning room door and immediately entered into the fray. Francisco yelled at his wife, "Go get help...Lacoya, go find the Captain of the Guard. Quick! Take these women out of here to safety. Quickly, go now!" Lacoya Ines with a frightened look turned quickly to the guests and escorted them out through the kitchen door entrance. They ran down a hallway toward the outside terrace. Two more of the Men of Chile appeared in the terrace doorway with their swords pointed at the women and blocking their way.

"Stay where you are or you will all die this instant!" said one dark haired conquistador.

"What do you want? Why are you here? Why are you doing this?" The cries of the captured women and unarmed guests where adding to the confusion.

"Silence! Go back to the dinning room!" ordered the conquistador.

The battle continued with Francisco and his two armed companions giving a good account of themselves each battling two of the intruders. Francisco blocked another blow and with his sword pushed one conquistador against the other. Pizarro quickly slashed the unfortunate soldier just under his protecting maile and across his stomach. With another thrust of his sword the second conquistador was run through. Francisco looked up just in time to see the last of his friends that had come to his Sunday dinner party breathe his final breathe as two of the young warriors overpowered the old gentleman. Francisco picked up the closest chair and tossed it at the attackers. Another group of conquistadors entered the Governor's dining room led by a young dark-skinned man dressed in a fine coat of shinning armor wearing a Spanish helmet with a superb red parrot's feather. He was obviously their leader. "Ah hah! Finally, I have you. I will have my revenge...Francisco!"

The pause interrupted this battle momentarily as everyone watched the verbal exchange between the leaders of the empire of Peru with anticipation. "So, Diego de Almagro the Younger, you dare come into my house like a thief in the night? What do you want here? Do you possibly think that you will get away with this intrusion and this murderous act? I will see that you are all hung for this outrage. You will die for this!"

"No, my esteemed Governor," said Diego haughtily. "You will die tonight, just like your brothers killed my father. You robbed him and then murdered him. He was your partner and your best friend. You turned on him and then you killed him! I am only seeking my own justice and right to rule this people in my father's place!"

"So, come ahead! I will give you your chance to take what isn't yours!" Francisco raised up his sword and ran the few steps toward Diego. Francisco's first blow glanced off his opponent's sword as Diego defended himself. Diego slipped and fell backward, and Francisco closed in for the final blow. Diego was not expecting such an attack by the old warrior. Two of Diego's comrades quickly pushed the tall, slim old gentleman away. Diego the Younger was on his feet immediately, anger red upon his face.

"Stay away from him…He is mine!" Diego knocked away his friend's hand that had been offered in help. Diego threw away his shield and picked up his sword from the ground and made three quick slashing blows in anger which Francisco easily defended and blocked. Francisco showed his skill with a quick downward glancing move that startled Diego as it cut him deeply on the arm. Diego the Younger cried out in painful anguish and dived under the table to protect himself. Two conquistadors started into the conflict to distract Francisco from continuing his purpose of dispatching their leader, Diego the Younger. Francisco defended himself and started to attack these new pursuers. Diego the Younger stood up a little dazed holding his injured arm and wincing in pain. "I will kill you for this!" Diego murmured.

"You are a coward and a snake coming into my house and killing my friends. Come let us finish this fight, just the two of us." Francisco was a commanding courageous figure of a man even when surrounded on all sides by the enemy. Pizarro blocked the swords of his assailants and pushed them aside. Francisco turned and rushed three steps toward Diego the Younger. A conquistador standing close to the renegade leader stepped in front and took Francisco's first blow and then countered with one of his own. Diego with his good sword arm pushed the young man into Francisco from behind. The sudden move unbalanced and distracted the young conquistador. Pizarro with the advantage thrust his sword through the man. Diego the Younger continued pushing his dying companion further onto Francisco's sword and toward him. Pizarro was unable to step backwards quickly enough to extract the sword from the dead man, and Diego brought his sword up high and slashed Francisco across his neck and chest. Francisco fell to the floor mortally wounded. "Oh....dear God!"

Instantly, Lacoya Ines ran to his side pushing everyone else to the side. Tears cursed down her cheeks and she looked up at Diego and hissed, "You madmen, you have killed my husband...You have killed the governor!" she cried uncontrollably. "God help us!"

Monica sat up with a start. "Peter was right! According to history, Francisco Pizarro was murdered in his governor's palace in Lima! Why had they then seen his mummified remains in the Royal Chamber seated on the golden throne in the secret tunnel?" Monica wondered to herself. "And what happened to all of his treasure and fortune that he supposedly collected? How did it get to Cusco? If Francisco is not buried and displayed in his tomb here in his Cathedral in Lima, who is buried there?"

"Mother, are you awake?" Monica whispered as she looked over at her mother. "We need to talk!" She motioned to the bathroom with her head. For the next hour with the water running in the sink and in the shower, Eva Rodriguez explained and taught her daughter several important truths that were part of their Inca heritage and registered on the knotted quipu. "Mother, why can't you tell me everything from the 'Sacred Quipu'? I am ready to learn. I need to know everything. Please, Mother….Please tell me," Monica pleaded.

"Monica, I know I can trust you and that you are ready. But I am worried that they mean to kill us, or at least me. I think that the less you know the better for the time being. The evil purposes of these men have not fully been revealed to us. So, I think if you do not know anything then you will hopefully survive and be able to learn about it latter."

"But, Mother, how is that possible?" asked Monica. "You are the 'Rememberer' and the only one who knows all the details and the history of the Sacred Quipu.

"As long as the Sacred Quipu survives and you guard it with your life, the Inca Priests in Cusco can help you. They know the key to the knots and how to read the Sacred Quipu. They do not know what is to be remembered and the facts, because they have never seen it or studied it. There are other ancient quipu and they have the key to translating

247

the Sacred Quipu knots that has been handed down in our family from generation to generation. If I do not survive and they kill me, it will not matter, because you can still learn to be the chosen 'rememberer.'"

Monica started to cry. "Mother do you think that they will kill us? Why are they doing this?" Monica sobbed.

"It is always all about money. Your Uncle Carlos wants all the power and glory of the Inca people, but what he most especially wants is the wealth. The treasure and gold is what they seek. I am not going to give it to them. I would rather die first!"

"Mother what are you saying?" asked Monica.

"I guess I am saying that there is treasure. Francisco Pizarro was not buried in his tomb here in Lima, but Lacoya Ines took his body back to her beloved Cusco. Another old conquistador's body was purposely switched and buried in his place. She poisoned herself to die and be with him forever in the secret tunnel after she hid the treasure. I don't want to tell you anymore, but it is all part of the teachings of the 'Sacred Quipu.'"

"There is more treasure?" queried Monica incredulously.

Eva Rodriguez just looked at her daughter with a smile. "Yes... Lacoya Ines couldn't risk transporting it back to Cusco, so she hid it! We have been waiting for generations, for centuries to give it back to the Incan people. To use it to make them a strong and powerful people once again. I thought maybe the time had come, when Peter and the University of California came up with this plan, and that maybe it might be possible. I spoke to two of the Incan Elders about the possibilities by phone before we left California. They agreed that maybe now was the time and that we should pursue this plan with secrecy and with caution. We realize that this is the largest and most incredible treasure the world has ever known. Its secrets have been carefully safeguarded for centuries. Our people need this important financial help, now. They are in poverty. It is important that they get a chance to benefit from it. We have had many corrupt political and military regimes that would have taken the treasure unto themselves and squandered it. The time has never been right before. Now, finally, when it appeared like we had the right time and opportunity; we are captured before our mission even started. Your uncle could spoil everything. And I don't trust him, or want to tell him anything. Now, I'm tired and I have told you too much…And lots more than I wanted to or that I should have told you. I love you…It's late…. Let's go to bed."

Chapter Notes – Chapter 26

Francisco Pizarro was killed in his own governor's mansion in the capital city of Lima on the fateful day of July 26th 1541 at the approximate age of 71 (He never knew his own birthday). Actually, there is some dispute as to the date of his death. Many history books use July 26th as his death date other sources use June 26th as the proper date. In the Spanish language the difference is only one letter (Julio or Junio). On his new tomb made in 1985 in Lima, historians have used June 26th 1541 as the date. He was murdered by remnants of his own men and old friend, Diego de Almagro, as he sat at supper. These 'Men of Chile' as they were called, ruled Peru until overpowered by the army of Gonzalo Pizarro, Francisco's younger brother.

There is a good possibility that more than one treasure cache actually exists in Peru today because of the weight and bulkiness of golden treasure. It was very difficult to transport in caravans by pack animals through the mountains, and easy prey for bandits. So, in most cases it was easier to hide or bury the treasure close to where it was found.

Main Plaza in Lima, Peru

Chapter 27

University of California – Present Day

"Professor Nelson, it has now been almost three weeks and nobody has heard from them at all. Something is wrong…I can feel it. I've tried to talk to everyone that I could think of calling. No one has heard from them! They did not get back to Cusco!" said Peter emphatically.

"Wow! There has got to be some kind of logical explanation to this. People just can't vanish into thin air. Maybe Monica stopped in Lima to spend some time with friends there on the way home," questioned the professor calmly.

"I don't think so…I just talked to the receptionist where Monica works at the Department of Tourism. She told me that Monica had phoned her from California and told them that they were coming home early. Then, a day later she had to phone back and say that she wouldn't be back to work right away. Monica said that she would need one more extra day off, because she had some meetings with the University of California. They never reached Cusco, never got home at all!" Peter was just about to blow a gasket. He was red in the face and exasperated by the whole affair. No one seemed to care that they were gone, vanished into thin air.

"Well, phone the police there, again. I will make a call to the FBI and make sure that they were on the plane and have left the country," promised Professor Nelson. The old scientist then turned around and walked out the door. Two other grad students were listening to the whole affair and looked on with blank faces. Peter shared this small office with no windows with three other grad students. It had two desks back to back and four chairs. They did have two computers and two phones, but everything had to be shared. The room had originally been designed to be a storage room and they were lucky to have any office accommodations at all. Peter only rated an office because he was teaching a lab class for Professor Nelson, so he wasn't complaining. A lot of grad students never did get to have an office to work from. Immediately, Peter was dialing on the phone again. This time he dialed the number of his military acquaintance, General Rojas. Peter thought that maybe he had been stonewalled by the police, and the general might be able to find out something for him.

How could this be? Peter's own father, Don Jose, had driven Monica and Eva Rodriguez to the airport. He had stayed at the ticket counter and made sure that their suitcases were checked in and that they had received their boarding passes before he had even said goodbye. So, Don Jose was sure that they had gotten on the plane. They were there early and had plenty of time to get through security and down to their gate of departure. Peter couldn't figure it out. He had phoned the police department in Cusco over a week ago and filed a missing person's report. Peter had already contacted them twice since then and they could tell him nothing. Peter was pretty certain that they had not returned to

Cusco. The lady managing the restaurant had not heard from Eva either, which was really strange.

"General Rojas…Hi, this is Peter Martin from California. Hi, sorry to call you, but I don't know who else to talk to. It seems I'm always bringing my problems to you," began Peter.

"That's fine…how can I help you in California? My helicopter gun ships can't fly that far!" laughed the general.

"No…no…it's nothing like that. Monica and her mother Eva Rodriguez came to California to visit me. They returned to Lima by plane, but never arrived in Cusco. I have filed a missing person's report with the police, but I am getting nowhere. It has been almost three weeks and I am very worried that something terrible has happened to them." Peter said as he quickly explained the situation to the general.

"Well, maybe they stopped off in Lima to visit friends or something," answered General Rojas.

"No, I don't think so, general….It's been too long and Monica and her mother were both due back to work more than two weeks ago. Could you please phone Aero Peru for me and find out if they actually arrived in Lima and if they got on a flight to Cusco? Aero Peru won't release any information about its passengers to me. Could you please help me?" begged Peter. "I think the 'Shinning Path' must be involved again. I think Monica has been kidnapped with her mother!"

"Amazing....Peter I didn't know that two young people could get into so much trouble. I'll look into it, and have my staff do some investigation. Give me some phone numbers where I can reach you," said the general.

"Thanks...," " was all that Peter could respond. He was getting emotional and choking up. Finally, he was talking to someone that was interested in trying to help and someone that Peter had confidence in. Peter gave him phone numbers and finished his phone call. He leaned back in his chair. "Whew! This is getting intense," Peter exclaimed out loud. A realization that the Shinning Path terrorist group could be involved in another abduction, had dawned on Peter previously. But now, Peter was almost convinced that it was true. Why did they want to capture Monica again? Did someone else know about the treasure? Did someone else know that Eva Rodriguez was the Inca Queen? What did they hope to gain by another kidnapping? Was this only about money or was there another reason that Monica and her mother were being targeted? The questions just kept pouring in. Peter had not slept well for days. It was worrying him sick. Now that he had explained the whole terrorist experience to his parents last week, they were worried sick as well. Peter asked his father if he could loan him some money to go back to Peru and find them. The answer was an emphatic 'yes' with no questions. They wanted to know more about what happened and exactly what his feelings for Monica were. Peter did not want to tell them any more about the terrorists. He admitted that he had grown very fond of Monica, but that she was always in trouble. So, he did not think that it would be a very good plan to marry such a girl. But, he did feel a responsibility to go help her, now. Peter was trying to cover his tracks and he had to tell some small white lies to keep his parents from asking too many questions.

"Professor Nelson, I have talked to the police again and now the military. So far, no one can tell us a thing!" Peter was back in his professor's long narrow office reporting on his progress or lack thereof. "What else can we do?" asked Peter.

"Well, Peter we have finally had confirmation through the FBI that Monica and Eva were on the airline flight to Peru. So they definitely left the country and are now back in Peru," confirmed Professor Nelson.

"I've got to go down there, professor! I've got to find them!" exclaimed Peter.

"Well, I have just received word from the department chairman that we are going to get full funding for this project and the university will buy the building that we need and everything. So, next month after you graduate then we will send you down with a team to Cusco to get things started and you can look for them then. It looks like I won't be going down until later. We will just have to be patient and see what the police can turn up."

"No…professor, I can't wait. I must go now. My parents will give me the money. They will support me and help me financially. I have to find them and find out what happened," said Peter emphatically.

"But, Peter, it is in the middle of the semester, you are teaching my lab class. You are due to graduate in a month. You can't go now," explained the professor. Peter hung his head down low. He was utterly dejected and discouraged. Professor Nelson could see the disappointment on his face. "What if they have met with some sort of foul play…heaven forbid....What if you get involved in it? Peter it is too dangerous, we had better let the police handle it."

"Professor, you don't understand I have to find her...She may be in danger. I need to go down there, now!" said Peter hoarsely. "I have to find her!"

"Peter, you can't throw everything away, now. Just wait until after the semester, until after graduation. We'll get the project planned and we will select a good team and all go down together with a proper exploration and university sponsored project."

Peter leaned down to look his professor directly into his face. He could feel a couple of tears rolling down his cheeks. That seemed odd to him. He could not remember having tears trickle down from his eyes since he was a kid. He had never told anyone of his feelings here at the university about Monica, before. Professor Nelson had noticed a change in the relationship between Peter and Shelley since Shelley had announced her engagement to the whole department. Peter could feel a swelling sensation rising up into his breast as he looked directly into the eyes of this wonderful old man. "I love her. I need to go to her and find her." It was a simple enough expression. Professor Nelson just nodded. With that small gesture, Peter wheeled around and exited his office. Peter couldn't believe it. Had he really admitted to Professor Nelson that he loved Monica? Had he really admitted to himself and finally acknowledged to himself that he loved this black-haired Peruvian Princess? He couldn't believe it. He was going to throw everything in his life away, all the years and hard work, to go and find her.

Peter took the elevator to the ground level of the building and ran outside. He burst out of the large glass doors of the lobby and onto the grass courtyard in between buildings. There were hundreds of students walking past him in both directions, but Peter didn't care. Peter threw his arms up into the air, heavenward, and yelled, "I love you Monica."

Chapter Notes – Chapter 27

No notes.

About the Author

L. Norman Shurtliff, (Les) was born in St. George, Utah and grew up on a small vegetable farm in Southern Nevada. Les was able to serve a mission for the LDS Church in Argentina for two years where he learned the Spanish language and the culture of the wonderful people of South America. He attended Brigham Young University and received a Bachelor of Science Degree in 1979. Immediately after graduation from university the family moved to the small town of Taylor, B.C. Les got a job at the local oil refinery as a chemist and has been an oil field scientist for the past twenty-eight years.

After his mission nearly 30 years ago Les was able to visit and see first hand the magical land of the Incas. Intrigued with the history and culture of South America, Les has visited this land of beauty and mystery many times since and continues to search this land for its many types of treasure. The gold may now be gone or only found in museums, but there are still other kinds of treasure more important that can only be found in the wonderful people who live in this enchanted land. The author has spent a lifetime studying and visiting South America and has a unique passion for this people and their legends. The evidence of this passion is seen in the long hours and effort to write a novel which will bring to life the story of a "chosen and elect" people.

Les and his wife, Christal have four sons and three daughters and continue to live in Taylor, B.C. His real passion is to visit South America during the cold winter months in Canada and thus escape to a land where dreams really have come true.

CPSIA information can be obtained at www.ICGtesting.com
Printed in the USA
BVOW07s0944180914

367299BV00001B/5/P